BUZZ AROUND THE TRACK

They Said It

"I've been waiting most of my life for this opportunity. Jake McMasters is going to help me find out who I am."
—Becky Peters

"Sometimes hope can be cruel, but false hope can be even worse. It's always better to know the truth. That's why I agreed to take Patsy Grosso's case…and now Becky's."
—Jake McMasters

"My baby girl was taken from me, and I want to know what happened to her."
—Patsy Grosso

"Patsy is sure that Gina is still alive somewhere…. Yes, I want to know the truth, but more than that, I want to keep my wife from getting her heart broken."
—Dean Grosso

INGRID WEAVER

believes that romance stories are the country music of popular fiction. They're entertaining, fun, yet packed with emotions that touch the heart. Recipient of a Romance Writers of America's prestigious RITA® Award, as well as a *Romantic Times BOOKreviews* Career Achievement Award, Ingrid lives on a farm near Toronto, where she's working on her next book.

NASCAR

WITHIN STRIKING DISTANCE

Ingrid Weaver

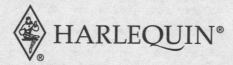

HARLEQUIN®

TORONTO • NEW YORK • LONDON
AMSTERDAM • PARIS • SYDNEY • HAMBURG
STOCKHOLM • ATHENS • TOKYO • MILAN • MADRID
PRAGUE • WARSAW • BUDAPEST • AUCKLAND

If you purchased this book without a cover you should be aware that this book is stolen property. It was reported as "unsold and destroyed" to the publisher, and neither the author nor the publisher has received any payment for this "stripped book."

Recycling programs for this product may not exist in your area.

ISBN-13: 978-0-373-18526-9

WITHIN STRIKING DISTANCE

Copyright © 2009 by Harlequin Books S.A.

Ingrid Weaver is acknowledged as the author of this work.

NASCAR® and the NASCAR Library Collection® are registered trademarks of the National Association for Stock Car Auto Racing, Inc.

All rights reserved. Except for use in any review, the reproduction or utilization of this work in whole or in part in any form by any electronic, mechanical or other means, now known or hereafter invented, including xerography, photocopying and recording, or in any information storage or retrieval system, is forbidden without the written permission of the publisher, Harlequin Enterprises Limited, 225 Duncan Mill Road, Don Mills, Ontario, Canada M3B 3K9.

This is a work of fiction. Names, characters, places and incidents are either the product of the author's imagination or are used fictitiously, and any resemblance to actual persons, living or dead, business establishments, events or locales is entirely coincidental.

This edition published by arrangement with Harlequin Books S.A.

® and TM are trademarks of the publisher. Trademarks indicated with ® are registered in the United States Patent and Trademark Office, the Canadian Trade Marks Office and in other countries.

www.eHarlequin.com

Printed in U.S.A.

NASCAR HIDDEN LEGACIES

The Grossos

Dean Grosso
m.
Patsy Clark Grosso

— Kent Grosso
(fiancée Tanya Wells)

— Gina Grosso
(deceased)

— Sophia Grosso
(fiancé Justin Murphy)

Dean's best friend

The Claytons

Steve Clayton ⑩

— Mattie Clayton ⑭

Damon Tieri ⑪

Business partner

The Clarks

Andrew Clark
(divorced)

Patsy's brother

Garrett Clark ⑯
(Andrew's stepson)

Patsy's cousin

Jake McMasters ⑧

Kent's agent

Kane Ledger ⑦

The Cargills

Alan Cargill (widower)

Nathan Cargill ⑤

The Branches

Maeve Branch
(div. Hilton Branch) m.
Chuck Lawrence

— Will Branch ②

— Bart Branch

— Penny Branch m.
Craig Lockhart

— Sawyer Branch
(fiancée
Lucy Gunter)

① *Scandals and Secrets*
② *Black Flag, White Lies*
③ *Checkered Past*
④ *From the Outside*
⑤ *Over the Wall*
⑥ *No Holds Barred*
⑦ *One Track Mind*
⑧ *Within Striking Distance*
⑨ *Running Wide Open*
⑩ *A Taste for Speed*
⑪ *Force of Nature*
⑫ *Banking on Hope*
⑬ *The Comeback*
⑭ *Into the Corner*
⑮ *Raising the Stakes*
⑯ *Crossing the Line*

THE FAMILIES AND THE CONNECTIONS

The Sanfords

Bobby Sanford
(deceased)
m.
Kath Sanford

— Adam Sanford ①

— Brent Sanford ⑫

— Trey Sanford ⑨

The Hunts

Dan Hunt
m.
Linda (Willard) Hunt
(deceased)

— Ethan Hunt ⑥

— Jared Hunt ⑮

— Hope Hunt ⑫

— Grace Hunt Winters ⑯
(widow of Todd Winters)

The Mathesons

Brady Matheson
(widower)
(fiancée Julie-Anne Blake)

— Chad Matheson ③

— Zack Matheson ⑬

— Trent Matheson
(fiancée Kelly Greenwood)

The Daltons

Buddy Dalton
m.
Shirley Dalton

— Mallory Dalton ④

— Tara Dalton ①

— Emma-Lee Dalton

PROLOGUE

June 1978

"DADDY, YOU HAVE to help me. Please."

"Cynthia, we should tell the police."

"No! We can't do that. Promise me you won't. No one can find out what happened. My life would be ruined. Please, Daddy, don't tell anyone!"

Lightning flickered through the rain-streaked window panes, probing the tiny apartment as if to spotlight the evidence of what Cynthia had done. Gerald scanned the mess one final time, then turned his attention to the infant that squirmed in his daughter's arms.

The baby's face was flushed red and her mouth was trembling. So far, her sobs had been too weak for the neighbors to hear over the storm, but she looked as if she was about to start crying in earnest any minute. Whatever they decided to do, they needed to do it quickly.

"I made a mistake. I didn't mean any harm."

"I know you didn't, Cynthia." He heard his voice take on the soothing tone he always used when she was upset, even though in this case, he was aware that sympathy wasn't going to be enough. This was no minor misunderstanding that he could solve with a smile and some cash.

"The police would put me in jail. You can't let them do that. I'd die!"

Gerald pinched the bridge of his nose as he tried to reason this through. He knew what was right, yet his mind filled with the unthinkable image of his daughter locked in among hardened criminals. She was so full of life; prison would destroy her spirit. How could he do that to his only child?

"I don't know what came over me. I never meant to hurt anyone…but now it's too late to put things right."

He watched Cynthia jiggling the infant in her arms. His daughter was a grown woman, yet it seemed like only yesterday that she had been a baby and he'd been the one holding her. Thunderstorms had always frightened her, and he'd spent many nights rocking her to sleep. She'd been even younger than this child when her mother had died, less than one day old, and completely helpless. She'd needed him so much; she'd become the center of his world.

She still was.

The baby arched her back and finally let loose with a full-throated wail. Cynthia slapped her hand over the child's mouth, smothering the noise. "Shut up. Just *shut up*."

Gerald took the baby from her and lifted it to his shoulder. The change in position quieted her immediately. He was sure Cynthia hadn't meant to be rough. She was upset, and that was to be expected. She hadn't had any experience with babies. It would be different if the child was hers. Then she would feel the same powerful, all-encompassing, unconditional love he'd felt for her.

She'd be a wonderful mother. It wouldn't be fair if she was denied that possibility in the future because of one moment's poor judgment. Her fiancé wouldn't understand that everything Cynthia had done, she'd done because of her love for him. That man wouldn't be helping her—it was good that she'd called Gerald instead. No one understood her as well as her father did.

Cynthia shoved the coffee table back into place with her

foot and began stuffing the baby's paraphernalia into a diaper bag. "After I clean up here, maybe we could leave the child someplace. Then no one would have to know."

He rubbed his hand over the baby's back. He was sure Cynthia hadn't meant to be callous, either. She was distraught, that's all, and wasn't thinking things through. She'd always been an impulsive girl. "We can't simply abandon her," he said. "Aside from the risk to the baby, there would be an investigation once she was found. The truth of who she is might come out."

"No! We can't let that happen. My life would be over." Cynthia clutched his arm and tipped her face upward. Another flash of lightning strobed through the window, making the tears on her cheeks glisten. "You have to think of something. I love you, Daddy. Please, help me."

Gerald sighed. He had no defense against her tears. What was the point of punishing her for something she hadn't meant to do? No one was to blame for an accident. When she'd been five and had broken his late wife's favorite vase, he hadn't been capable of scolding her. She'd been upset enough already. It had been the same when she'd been sixteen and had hit the neighbors' dog with her new car. He'd bought another dog for them, a pedigreed champion that was better than the one they'd had. Everything had worked out well in the end.

Yes, he'd always helped her. That's what love was all about. She was no longer a child, yet she still counted on him. He had to come through for her; he couldn't let her down.

He looked from his daughter to the baby.

And slowly, a plan began to form.

CHAPTER ONE

June 2009

"MR. MCMASTERS?"

At the woman's voice, Jake paused to look around. It was noon, and the first sunny day after two days of rain, so even a small park like this one was busy. Half the benches beneath the trees were already occupied by people eating their lunches. A pair of men in suits brushed past him, using the sidewalk to cut through to the next street. That's where Jake had been headed, with the intention of hitting the corner diner and adding a nice, greasy burger to the three cups of coffee that had been his breakfast. He shaded his eyes against the sun, trying to see who had called him.

It didn't take any special detective skills to spot her. With her wide-brimmed yellow straw hat, neon pink blouse and billowing, yellow and pink flower-splotched skirt, she would stand out in any crowd.

The fact that she waved at him helped, too.

Jake rested both hands on his cane and studied her as she approached. She moved with the grace of a dancer, her long limbs slender and in perfect proportion to her height. He estimated she was only a couple of inches short of six feet, another reason she stood out among the lunching locals. And the closer she got, the more striking she looked.

No, *striking* was an understatement. This woman was a knockout. Absolutely beautiful.

And she looked familiar.

That didn't make sense. He was certain he had never met her before. He would have remembered if he had—any man who possessed a pulse would remember meeting this woman—yet he felt an unmistakable tickle of recognition.

"Mr. McMasters?" she repeated, stopping in front of him.

He nodded. "That's me."

"I apologize for chasing you down like this. I hadn't realized you closed your office for lunch. I meant to be there earlier but I was held up and by the time I got here it was already twelve and I must have just missed you. I was going back to my car when I guessed that must be you crossing the park and—" She stopped talking and pressed her palm flat against her midriff. She breathed deeply a few times before she extended her hand and smiled. "Sorry for rambling. Let me start over. I'm Becky Peters."

It didn't seem possible, but that smile made her look even more beautiful. It involved every part of her face, turning features that were already perfect into a harmony of…what? Honesty? Friendliness?

He was jumping to conclusions about her character. Aside from her outward appearance, he knew nothing about her. Realizing he was staring, he clasped the hand she offered.

And he was jarred by another round of recognition. Not from her name, but from her touch.

Her eyes were a warm, smoky blue. It was a memorable color, a shade that reminded him of a summer horizon at dusk. They widened slightly, as if she felt the same odd tickle from the contact of their palms that he did.

This was getting stranger by the minute. Jake leaned forward. "Miss Peters, have we met before?"

"No." The word came out rough. She cleared her throat. "No, we haven't met."

"Then how did you know who I was?"

"Mostly it was a lucky guess. I also asked my friend about you before I decided to come."

He returned his hand to his cane. Right. Sometimes he forgot about his most distinguishing characteristic. "I see. Is your friend a client of mine?"

"Not really." She looked past him. "You must have been on your way someplace. I hate to hold you up but I have to be at work later this afternoon, so would you mind if we talked now?"

His stomach did a little roll to remind him about the burger he'd promised it. He could ignore his hunger, but he couldn't afford to ignore potential business so he led the way to a vacant bench in the shade of a chestnut tree. He waited until the woman sat, then settled at an angle beside her, leaned his cane against the seat and stretched out his left leg. "It's lucky you caught up with me. Most days my work takes me out in the field. The only sure way to catch me in my office is to make an appointment."

"Of course. I should have guessed that a private investigator would be out, well, investigating."

"You must be anxious to employ my services."

"You have no idea." She took off her sun hat and laid it on her lap. "I've been waiting most of my life for this opportunity."

Jake allowed himself a few seconds to admire her hair. It was light brown, with streaks the color of honey. It flowed over her shoulders in lush waves, enough for a man to wrap around his fingers… He shifted on the bench to take his notebook from his pants pocket. "Which is?"

"Mr. McMasters, I want to find out who I am."

That makes two of us, he thought, pulling the stub of his

pencil from the notebook's spiral binding. The sense of familiarity was growing with each moment that passed. The name Peters didn't ring a bell. Maybe he'd known her under a different one. He checked her left hand but there was no wedding ring in sight. No tan line from one, either. "Perhaps you could explain further, Miss Peters."

"I was adopted. I tried to find my birth parents for years, but there aren't any official records of my adoption."

"And you want me to try my luck?"

"Yes. Well, there's more to it. I heard that you were already looking into the Gina Grosso case."

Not another one!

Jake scribbled a few words in his notebook to give himself a chance to cover his disappointment. Becky Peters hadn't struck him as a crank. But that could be because he hadn't been exactly objective in his assessment of her so far.

So she thought she was Gina Grosso? Well, welcome to the club. Forty-two women who claimed to be Gina had shown up at Jake's office since the story had gone public, but none of them had proven to be legitimate possibilities. They'd had various motives for making the claim. Some wanted a share of the Grossos' money, some wanted to bask in their fame. Who could blame them? The Grosso family was NASCAR royalty, which gave them star status here in Charlotte.

It hadn't always been that way. Thirty-one years ago, Dean and Patsy Grosso had been a pair of teenagers living on love and dreams of NASCAR glory. Patsy had given birth to twins at a Nashville hospital, a boy and a girl they named Kent and Gina, but the girl was abducted from the hospital nursery, supposedly by a ring that sold babies through private adoptions. All indications at the time had led the police to believe the infant had died, but a few months ago someone had started blogging about the incident, claiming that Gina Grosso was still alive.

Sometimes hope could be cruel, but false hope could be even worse. It was always better to know the truth. That was why Jake had agreed to take the case when his cousin Patsy had asked him, even though the FBI were looking into it, too. The Grosso family deserved to know what had really happened to their child.

Jake doubted whether the forty-two women he'd already met who'd thought they were Gina would have been so eager to claim a connection if Dean and Patsy had been anyone else. He flicked his pencil between his fingers and returned his gaze to the woman beside him. "Miss Peters, why do you believe you might be the missing Gina Grosso?"

She pressed her lips together, as if unsure how to proceed. Jake waited her out. When she did speak, her tone was hesitant. "I have no way of knowing for sure, but I honestly believe it's a possibility. I've thought about it since the story came out, but it seemed so…tabloid, I didn't want to say anything at first or I'd look like a crank."

Well, at least she was realistic. "You evidently changed your mind."

"Yes. That's why I came to you. Tara said that you've been checking out the information she gave you and that a lot of the facts that have been posted about Gina matches me."

"Who's Tara?"

"Tara Dalton, the friend I mentioned earlier."

That got his attention. Tara was a journalist who was writing a book about the prominent NASCAR families. She had come across the story about the missing Gina during the course of her research, and she was the one who had first alerted the family to the possibility that Gina might still be alive. She'd cooperated completely with Jake's investigation and had readily shared her source. Unfortunately, he hadn't been able to identify the anonymous blogger who was posting the information. The FBI had more clout than him when it came to tracking someone through cyberspace.

All right, he'd call Tara later. If she could vouch for her friend, maybe this woman wasn't like the others. "Tell me about these facts that you think may match."

"My blood type is B positive."

The blogger claimed that Gina's blood type was B positive, which was the same as Patsy Grosso's. Though the baby hadn't been tested before she'd been abducted, there was a good chance she shared her mother's type. "I hope you're aware that you have that in common with almost ten percent of the U.S. population," Jake pointed out.

"I was adopted as an infant the same summer that Gina went missing."

Score two more. "Go on."

"My father used to be a mechanic on a NASCAR team. My parents would have been in Nashville for a race the weekend Gina was abducted."

This time the notes he scribbled were real. "What are your adoptive parents' names?"

"Floyd and Lizzie Peters. My mother died sixteen years ago and my father moved to Australia after he remarried. He lives in Melbourne."

Her words were matter-of-fact, but Jake could hear the effort that took. It sounded as if she still missed her parents. Was that one of her reasons for hoping to find another set? "You said there were no records of your adoption?"

"No, none. When I first tried to find my birth parents, my adoptive parents were dead set against it. I'd assumed they were just sensitive about the adoption issue, and I didn't want to upset them, so I stopped looking."

He studied her openly. Her eyes were blue like Patsy Grosso's, although a bit brighter. Apart from the streaks in her hair, its color was similar to Patsy's, too. She was taller than either Dean or Patsy, but not as tall as Kent, Gina's twin. Taken individually, none of her facial features were exact copies of those of the Grossos, yet there was still that sense of familiarity about her...

Was that what he had felt when he'd first seen her? Maybe his subconscious had picked up on an overall family resemblance, and it had made him think he'd recognized her.

Or maybe lack of nourishment was causing him to imagine things.

Either way, it was his job to investigate every claim. "Could you give me a number where I can reach you, Miss Peters? And your father's number in Melbourne, if you have it with you?"

"It's in my directory," she said, pulling her phone from a pocket in the side of her skirt. She read out her father's number, then gave him both her cell and her home numbers. "Does this mean you're going to look into this for me?"

"I'll follow up on some things and get back to you in a few days. How's that?"

Her face moved into another smile. This one wasn't as broad as the first, yet it seemed even more genuine. "Oh, that's wonderful. Thank you so much."

She sure didn't look like a gold-digging crank. Her eyes shone with an eagerness that she didn't try to hide. And beneath her very grown-up beauty, she carried a hint of vulnerability, almost like...

Like a lost child searching for her way home.

That intrigued him. It also served to remind him of how young she was. He returned his notebook to his pocket, retrieved his cane and stood. "No problem. It's what the Grossos are paying me for."

She rose to her feet gracefully. Still smiling, she stepped toward him, bringing herself into his personal space. She was close enough for him to catch her scent. Gardenias. Lush, soft and feminine. And definitely not childlike.

His nostrils flared, but otherwise he remained motionless. Even though he knew that his brain had to be addled from hunger, it looked for all the world as if she were about to put her arms around him.

Her eyes widened, just as they had when he'd taken her hand, only they weren't touching each other this time. Not yet, anyway. But all he needed to do was lean toward her...

She stepped back fast, narrowly missing the front wheels of a baby carriage that a woman was pushing along the sidewalk. She apologized for the near collision, placed her sun hat on her head and continued to back away. Her cheeks reddened. "Uh, thanks again, Mr. McMasters."

Keep it casual, he told himself. She couldn't *really* have meant to hug him, could she? As a rule, gorgeous thirty-one-year-old women didn't go around throwing themselves at middle-aged men they had just met. At high noon in a public park. His blood sugar must be tanking. He lifted his free hand to his forehead in a two-fingered salute. "Miss Peters."

She turned and crossed the park. Her yellow hat, pink blouse and flowered skirt flashed in the sunshine like a parting smile. Once she reached the street, she headed for the row of parked cars in front of the building that housed his office. She didn't look back as she folded her tall frame into a red compact, for which Jake was grateful. He didn't want her to notice that he was still standing in the same spot where she'd left him and watching her like some pathetic, abandoned dog.

"Man, you need that burger," he muttered, turning away. He crossed the road and headed for the diner on the corner. Barely halfway there, he stopped dead and looked behind him. He thought he'd caught a glimpse of Becky Peters in the window of the clothing store he'd just passed.

That was impossible. He'd watched her get into a car on the next block. He retraced his steps anyway, needing to prove to himself he wasn't going insane.

No one was in the window, not even mannequins. The space was filled with glossy, life-size posters that hung like banners from the ceiling of the display space. The posters were all the same. They advertised jeans. And in the center of each one, a woman posed half turned away, with her hands on her hips and her long, honey-streaked hair flowing past her shoulders. Her eyes were the smoky blue of a summer horizon, and they sparkled in an eager—and familiar—smile. It was Becky Peters, all glammed up and more striking than ever.

Some detective he was. He passed this window at least four times a day but he'd never really looked at it. He had no idea how long the posters had been up, but even if they'd been hung this morning, they provided a logical explanation for the feeling of recognition that had been teasing him.

Now it made sense. Becky was a model. She had the height for it. She also had the slender figure and the perfect, symmetrical features that a camera would love. She'd be a natural. *This* was why he'd thought he'd met her before. He'd probably seen her face in countless ads. Nothing strange or mysterious about that.

All right, then. As for the rest of his reaction to her, well, he'd remedy that with a side order of fries.

BECKY GROPED in her bag for her keys as she reached the veranda. Light sparkled through the ground-floor windows of the white clapboard Victorian, along with the strains of something classical from her landlady's piano. Mrs. Krazowski must be in a good mood today, if the lively tempo was anything to go by. Great. That made two of them. Smiling, Becky took her time as she climbed the stairs to her apartment, enjoying the way the music mellowed as it bounced off the woodwork. She loved this old house. It had character, just like her landlady. Without missing a beat, the music switched from classical to boogie-woogie. Seconds later, it was accompanied by the faint sound of a ringing phone.

Becky unlocked her apartment door and rushed inside to grab her phone from the hall table before the answering machine could click on. "Hello?"

"Hi. You seem out of breath."

At the sound of Tara Dalton's voice, Becky felt a prick of disappointment. Which immediately made her feel guilty. Tara had been her best friend for most of her life, and she always loved to talk to her. Besides, Jake McMasters had said he would get back to her in a few days, not a few hours, so she should have known it wouldn't be him.

Now, if only she could get her pulse back down to normal. She dropped her bag and closed the door. "I just got home."

"Out of breath *and* late. Is it too much to hope you were on a date?"

"Yes."

"Really? You've been holding out on me. Who were you with?"

"I meant yes, it's too much to hope. The shoot ran late, that's all. The designer samples were only in size 0 and 2, so they kept me waiting while they scrambled around for a size 6. They had to courier one in."

Tara laughed. "And did you get the usual lectures about needing to lose weight?"

"Ooo, darling," Becky said, dropping into an imitation of the art director who'd been at the shoot, "if only you could get rid of another four inches from your hips, you'd be perfect." She snorted. "More likely I'd be in a hospital."

"That's one weird business you're in. I don't know how anyone could find fault with your figure."

Becky considered her looks a lucky accident of genetics, so she had never felt vain about them. "Thanks. At least it pays the bills." She perched on the arm of the couch and slipped off her shoes. The wood floor was refreshingly cool beneath her feet. It was another one of the reasons she loved this old building. "I'd worked with the photographer before, though, so he was fine about the delay. We're still on for the NASCAR Sprint Cup Series race on Sunday, right?"

"Well, that's one of the reasons I'm calling."

Becky heard the answer in Tara's change of tone. Tara and Becky, along with their friend, Dr. Nicole Foster, were track buddies. It didn't matter whether it was a race or a practice, they had been hanging out together for years. But Nicole was going to be on duty at the track infield care center this weekend, and now it sounded as if Tara was backing out, too. "Uh-oh."

"No, I'm not bailing. Adam and I are going up to New Hampshire together and we'd like you to come with us."

"That's sweet of you to ask, but you don't need a third wheel."

"Then I'll tell him I'll meet him at the track later."

"Don't you dare. If I am ever lucky enough to be as much in love with a man as you are with Adam Sanford, I wouldn't want to waste a minute without him."

"Becky…"

"I might be late anyway." Her gaze went to the shelf of plants near her window. One of the ferns needed repotting. "I have a ton of stuff to get caught up on this weekend." She carried her phone back to the door and dug through the bag that she'd dropped. "And no offense, but I'd rather watch the race with your parents than with the owner of Sanford Racing. He wouldn't appreciate me rooting for Cargill-Grosso."

Tara laughed. "Adam wouldn't mind."

Becky grabbed a bottle of water from her bag, unscrewed the cap and took a long swallow. "Tara, I'm your friend, and I'm trying to let you off the hook so you can concentrate on the man you love. Take the gift, okay?"

"Thanks, Becky. You are a good friend. I'll ask Adam to

get garage passes for you and my parents, okay? It'll make me feel less guilty."

"You don't need to do that."

"Oh, if you don't want one—"

"Are you nuts? Of course I do. But I'm still not going to root for Sanford."

Tara chuckled. "Speaking of Cargill-Grosso, there's another reason I called. I heard you contacted Jake McMasters."

Her pulse gave an odd bump at the sound of Jake's name. It was the same kind of bump she'd felt when she'd heard the phone ringing. She took another gulp of water. "Yes, I met him this afternoon. How did you know?"

"He called me to verify who you were."

"That makes sense. I mentioned your name. He probably would want to know if I was on the level before he started investigating my adoption."

"Wow. So it's not just us. He thinks you could be Gina, too. That must have made you happy."

Happy? Sure, she was so happy that she'd almost hugged him. Becky returned to the couch and curled into one corner.

"Becky? Is something wrong?"

"Why didn't you tell me what he looks like?"

"What? I did."

"You told me he's tall and walks with a cane."

"That's right."

"You could have warned me that he's like a cross between George Clooney and Harrison Ford."

"Jake McMasters, private investigator?" Incredulity made Tara's voice rise. "Are we talking about the same man? He doesn't look anything like either of them."

Becky put down her water bottle and picked up a throw cushion to hug against her chest. She called up a mental image of Jake, which was easy to do since his face had been popping into her mind since she'd left him.

Tara was right. Jake didn't resemble either movie star. His face was lean and his jaw was square, but he could never be called leading-man handsome. By most standards, he wasn't good-looking at all. His nose was crooked, as if it had been broken at least once. A few faint traces of what had likely been teenage acne pitted the skin in the hollows of his cheeks. His hairline had receded at the corners of his forehead, and he apparently preferred to style his hair with his fingers rather than a comb.

Yet his gaze was steady and direct, something she didn't often see when she met a man for the first time. She'd had the feeling that he'd been trying to look past her outward appearance. Though he hadn't smiled, she had noticed laugh lines around his light blue eyes and the hint of a dimple at one corner of his mouth. Becky knew all too well how arbitrary a standard beauty could be. She had worked beside some of the most beautiful people in the world and had become immune to their effect years ago. She'd learned that pretty wrappings didn't necessarily mean the contents of the package were any good.

"It's not his features I meant," she said finally. "It's the impression he gives."

"I don't follow."

"He's like the characters those guys play. Strong. Solid and trustworthy. A man who isn't perfect but who does the right thing anyway."

"That must have been some meeting."

Becky could feel warmth seep into her cheeks. How could she explain the connection she'd felt to Jake when she didn't understand it herself? She hugged the pillow more tightly. "He appeared to take me seriously, which is a good start."

"I'm glad. I know how much finding your birth family means to you."

"I just hope he can learn something."

"He struck me as very competent. Dean and Patsy trust him, and not just because he's family."

"Do you mean he's a Grosso?"

"No, he's related to Patsy's side of the family. A distant cousin or something."

A cousin? Becky nibbled her lower lip. If she did turn out to be Gina Grosso, then Jake would be a blood relative. "How distant?"

"Very. Why?"

"I got this odd feeling when I met him, as if we had a connection. Do you think it could be because we're related?"

"I don't know. I suppose anything's possible."

Anything? Becky hoped that was true. It had seemed like such a long shot when she'd first considered the possibility that she might be Gina. Now that she'd taken the leap and had approached Jake, the idea was becoming more real.

That must be the reason she was feeling this low-level excitement whenever she thought of him. From the day Becky had learned she wasn't born to Floyd and Lizzy Peters, she had always dreamed of finding out who she really was. It was only natural that she'd be impressed by the man who could make her dream come true.

JAKE YAWNED, shut down his computer, then rocked back in his chair and propped his feet on his desk. The dentist and his patients next door had cleared out at dinnertime. The accountant across the hall had slammed her door two hours after that and clicked her high heels down the stairs. The cleaning crew had already come and gone, so aside from the lazy *shush* of the ceiling fan and the hum of the air conditioner in the window behind him, the building was quiet. Perfect time to sort through what he'd learned this week.

Only, it hadn't been much. More an absence of information, which in itself said a lot.

Rebecca Peters didn't have a record, unlike several of the previous Gina claimants. Not that he expected her to, although as a professional he shouldn't have had any expectations one way or the other. It had been easy to trace her life, since she'd gone to school here in Charlotte. She had begun working as a model before she graduated high school. Catalogue work mostly, rather than high-fashion catwalk stuff. She lived alone. He didn't know whether she was dating anyone.

Not that the last fact should matter. Her love life wasn't Jake's concern. His gaze strayed to the magazine on the corner of his desk. The ad on the back cover was the same picture of Becky as the one on the clothing store posters. He couldn't claim it had caught his eye as he'd gone past the newsstand, because all the magazines had been racked facing outward. No, he'd found it because he'd looked.

It was useful to have a picture of someone he was investigating. He usually had to take one himself with a telephoto lens. Too bad the impact of the polished, posed, made-up Becky in the ad didn't come close to the woman who had smiled at him in the park.

He rubbed his face. More than four days had passed since they'd met and the impression she'd made on him hadn't yet faded. He should stop staring at her picture, go home and get some sleep. But first, he needed to make a phone call. He cocked his wrist to check his watch, did some quick math to calculate the time difference with Australia, then pulled his feet off his desk and sat forward.

He'd gone as far as he could with the background check. Apart from her father, Becky Peters had no living relatives from her adoptive family Jake could interview. He reached Floyd Peters's cell phone on the fourth ring.

Unlike his adoptive daughter, Peters didn't sound open or friendly. His voice was curt as he confirmed who he was, each syllable bitten off as if he begrudged the breath it cost him.

"Mr. Peters, my name is Jake McMasters. I'm calling you from Charlotte with respect to your daughter, Becky."

"Is she all right? Are you a doctor?"

Jake paused. Peters's tone had changed instantly from gruff to anxious. He cared about his daughter, that was plain.

There were many approaches Jake could use to gain information. Unlike a cop, he didn't have to worry about the means he employed, since he wasn't concerned about building a court case. If he claimed to be a doctor and said it was a matter of life and death that Becky find a blood relative for a donor, he might be able to trick Peters into telling him who her birth parents were.

But aside from being a despicable trick to play on any parent, that ruse would fall apart as soon as Jake got off the phone and Peters called his daughter. Once that happened, there would be no hope of getting any further cooperation from him, regardless of the means.

Jake elected to go with honesty. "She's fine. I'm not a doctor, I'm a private investigator."

"Oh? I can't believe she'd be in any trouble. That's not like Becky."

"No, she isn't in trouble. On the contrary, she's very pleased I've agreed to help her."

"Help her do what?"

"You adopted Becky when she was an infant, isn't that right?"

There was a pause. In the background, Jake could hear the noise of an air wrench and the sharp, echoing thud of metal clunking onto metal. It sounded as if Peters was in a garage, which was to be expected. Becky had said he used to be a NASCAR mechanic.

When Peters spoke, his voice had cooled once more. "Yes, that's right."

"It's important to her to trace her roots. I'm looking into her adoption."

"Can't help you."

"Mr. Peters—"

"No. I'm her father, and my late wife was her mother. We were the only real parents she had."

"I've handled searches like this before. I assure you there's no need to be concerned. Your daughter's feelings for you won't change when she does learn who her biological parents were."

"There's no reason to stir up the past."

"It's Becky's past, Mr. Peters. Doesn't she have the right to know?"

"There's nothing to know."

"Apparently there were no official records of the adoption. You didn't go through an established agency. Was it a private adoption?"

"I already told her to let this go. She's throwing away her money."

Jake had no intention of telling Peters that it was the Grossos who were paying his bill. If the Peters were in on Gina's abduction, that was the surest way to make him clam up. Well, clam up worse.

"Your daughter appears to be an intelligent woman and is fully aware of what she's doing," Jake said. "Her desire to know her genetic background could become important to her health in later years." All right, he was hitting just a shade low of the belt, but it was the truth. "As a parent, don't you want what's best for her?"

Another pause, this one longer than the first. "I love my daughter, Mr. McMasters, and the best thing for Becky is to leave this alone."

"I'm afraid I can't do that, Mr. Peters. I'm being paid to learn the truth."

"You're wasting your time."

Jake swallowed his impatience. He didn't believe it would do any good to push Peters further. Not over the phone, anyway. It would be too easy for him to—

"I need to get back to work. Don't bother calling me again."

—to hang up. Jake replaced the receiver in its cradle. It had been worth a shot. Becky had said her father had refused to tell her the truth, but Jake had hoped Peters might have responded differently if the questions had come from a professional rather than from his daughter.

At least he'd learned one thing from the phone call. Even without being there in person to see the man's face, Jake was positive that Peters was worried. His resistance to revealing the facts about Becky's adoption must stem from more than being an overly possessive adoptive parent.

Floyd Peters had come across as a man with a guilty conscience.

FLOYD DUCKED his head to check that the other bathroom stalls were empty, then locked himself in the one farthest from the door and took his phone out of his coveralls. His hand trembled as he punched in a string of numbers. He hadn't used the phone number in more than thirty years—a bargain was a bargain—but he hadn't forgotten it. It had been etched into his subconscious like an emergency lifeline, or like one of those fire alarms with the lever stored behind glass.

The long-distance clicks took forever before the connection was finally made. He rocked back and forth, the soles of his shoes squeaking against the tile floor, while he counted the rings. Pick up. *Pick up.*

The voice that came on wasn't the one he wanted. Floyd wiped his palm on his leg and switched the phone to his other ear. "I don't care what time it is. I need to speak to Gerald."

CHAPTER TWO

IF SHE COULD MANAGE IT without bumping into anyone or
falling over anything, Becky sometimes wished she could
walk through the infield before a race with her eyes closed.
Without the visual overload of color and motion, it would be
the only way her other senses would be able to get equal time.

There was simply too much to absorb. Already the tarry
smell of pavement warming in the sun mixed with mouth-
watering whiffs of hot cooking oil from the concession
stands. Underlying that were the lingering notes of gasoline
and exhaust. Even hours before race time, the air was thrum-
ming with the sound of revving engines. The crowd was
already beginning to arrive from the parking areas, many
pulling children's wagons loaded with coolers and kids.
Here at the New Hampshire track, the wagons ended up
locked to the perimeter fence, yet regardless of which track
on the circuit Becky went to, the atmosphere was the same.
And she loved it like a second home.

Becky had always assumed that her fondness for racing
came from attending races as a child. Once the cars took the
track, the noise and nonstop action drowned out the ordinary
troubles of day-to-day life. It was one of the few activities
both her parents had enjoyed, and she had good memories
of traveling with them to the tracks around Charlotte.

Yet lately she'd been wondering if her feelings went
deeper than that. If she truly was Gina Grosso, she would be

the child of a legendary NASCAR driver. The sport would be in her blood.

All week she'd been torn between excitement over the possibility of being Gina and fear that she was getting her hopes up for nothing. She didn't want to be disappointed, and she knew she should be cautious, yet today her excitement was winning. She'd met Sophia Grosso Murphy several times and thought they could be friends. What if they were sisters? Kent Grosso drove for the Cargill-Grosso team. When she cheered for him, she could be cheering for the man who might be her twin brother. Yet another reason her senses were on overload. Her steps had an extra spring to them as she moved toward pit road.

"Becky. Yoo-hoo!"

She recognized the voice and paused to turn around.

Bud and Shirley Dalton, Tara's parents, were walking toward her from the rows of souvenir trailers. Both in their sixties and equally robust, they had begun to resemble each other, as longtime married couples often do. Shirley attributed the success of their marriage to their shared interest in every aspect of NASCAR—they traveled from one track to another in their RV, never missing a race.

"Shirley. Bud." She gave each of them a quick kiss on the cheek. "I was hoping I'd run into you two before we get to the grandstand."

"If you want to find Bud, just look for whoever's selling diecasts." Shirley elbowed her husband. "I swear, the man has a collection that outweighs the behemoth we drove here."

Bud made a show of rubbing his ribs. "Ouch. Did you sharpen your elbows again this morning?"

"Have to do something to get your attention. The new eye shadow didn't work."

"Honey, how many times do I have to tell you that you can't improve on perfection?"

Becky smiled. There was no mistaking the love beneath the Daltons' banter. Their family made up a big part of Becky's childhood memories—like any best friends, she and Tara had treated each other's houses as their own. On the weekends, the Daltons had often parked their RV beside the Peters's camper so they could all watch the races together. There had been times when Becky had been younger that she used to wish she could have belonged to a large, loving family like theirs.

The Grosso family was even bigger than the Daltons. If Becky were Gina, she would get her wish about being part of a large family. As for whether they would be as loving as the Daltons, Becky would bet that they were. Why else would they be so eager to find their missing daughter?

"All right," Shirley said, propping her hands on her hips and leaning toward Becky. "What's going on?"

"What? Besides the race?"

"Something's put that glow on your face. You're looking more gorgeous than usual. Is it a man?"

For some reason, she immediately thought of Jake McMasters. She shook her head, both at Shirley's question and the mental image. "I'm not seeing anyone."

"Could have fooled me. You have that dreamy look, the kind before you find out he leaves his socks in balls, picks his teeth and snores."

Bud tapped his chest. "I don't snore."

"Shirley," Becky said, "I hate to disappoint you, but just because two of your daughters found their Mister Right doesn't mean it's an epidemic."

"Then what's got you so happy?"

"It's race day. Why shouldn't I be happy? So, Bud, what car did you buy?"

"You're changing the subject," Shirley said.

Becky nodded. "You bet. Bud, help me here."

He held up his palms. "Nope. This sounds like girl talk."

"Which you should be used to after raising three of them," Shirley said.

"That's why I know better than to get involved," he returned.

"Smart man." Shirley gave him a tender pat where she'd elbowed him earlier. "That's why I married you, in spite of the socks in balls."

"And here I thought it was my collection of diecasts."

Becky laughed and linked arms with them. "Come on, you two. Let's go have a look at the real things."

EARL BUCKLEY, with his snow-white, handlebar mustache and his cue-ball head, was a common sight around the NASCAR circuit. He'd worked on cars back in the days when they'd still raced on the beach at Daytona. He'd grudgingly retired on his doctor's orders ten years ago, but that hadn't stopped him from hanging around the garages at every track. This wasn't the first time Jake had sought him out for information. Earl might have trouble remembering what he had for breakfast or where he'd parked his pickup, but his memory for anything related to racing was downright encyclopedic, and he enjoyed any reason to share it.

"Sure, I remember Floyd Peters," Earl said. "Intense guy. Kept to himself."

"How was he with engines?"

"He was a good troubleshooter. Used to diagnose engines by listening to them." Earl waved a gnarled hand toward the bank of high-tech diagnostic equipment that sat at the far side of the garage space. "Not like today. Everything's plug in this and computerized that. Looks more like a hospital than a garage. What's next? A guy won't even need to get his hands dirty?"

Jake grunted an agreement. Though computers had become a convenient tool of his own trade, as well, he preferred working the old-fashioned way. He wore out more shoe leather than telephones. He kept his notes on paper rather than a hard drive. And people, like cars, were individuals. They responded best to a hands-on approach. "So, Floyd had a good ear?"

"Yeah. Wasn't his fault he never ended up on a winning team."

"Do you remember who he worked for thirty-one years ago?"

"Geez, let me think. In '78? That would have been Shillington's team."

"Shillington? I've never heard of him."

"Auto-parts guy from Indianapolis. He didn't last long, folded the team after only a few seasons."

"How come?"

"He wasn't really into it. Never got a good driver after Shanks quit."

"Who was Shanks?"

"Young fella. Name of Hank but everyone called him Shanks because he was skinny as a rail. Looked like he was an up-and-comer but instead he up and quit." He stabbed the air with his index finger. "Now I remember why Floyd kept to himself. He had a wife who used to light into him. Geez, she didn't care who was around when she had a bone to pick. She traveled the circuit with him so he never got a break until the year the kid came along." He laughed. "Guess ol' Floyd found a better way than talking to take her mind off his faults."

So, Floyd and Lizzie Peters had a volatile relationship, Jake thought. Interesting.

"Hey, that was in '78, too," Earl said. "Had to be. Everyone was talking about Shanks quitting and Shillington getting out and there was Floyd, showing off baby pictures like he didn't have a care in the world. He didn't worry. He was good enough to get a job anywhere. Just bad luck that he never signed on with a winner."

"It sounds as if he was pleased about the baby."

"Sure. Kept his wife happy and at home for the second half of the season."

The second half? That agreed with what Becky had told him, that she had been adopted during the summer. Jake wouldn't expect Earl to have noticed that Floyd's wife hadn't appeared pregnant. That kind of detail wouldn't have stuck in his mind because it wasn't directly related to cars. Depending on Lizzie's weight to begin with, it might have gone unnoticed anyway. "Do you remember when the baby arrived?"

Earl pinched one end of his mustache and rubbed it between his fingers as he thought. "I don't know exactly. We were working for different teams. I just remember him showing the pictures."

"Okay."

"Poor Floyd. I haven't seen him around since the mid-eighties. Probably got a job that let him stay home with his family more, but I don't know why he'd want to. Wonder if his wife nagged him to death…" Earl's words trailed off as he looked past Jake's shoulder. "Huh, she looks familiar."

Jake planted the tip of his cane and half pivoted so he could scan the crowd. The public area of the garage was rapidly filling with fans after autographs and pictures. No one appeared to be paying any attention to the two of them. "Who do you mean?"

"Over near the doorway. That girl in the blue No. 414 shirt. She reminds me of somebody."

Even before Earl had finished the description, Jake had spotted her. Becky Peters was as easy to notice in a busy garage as in a sun-filled park or a store window. She wasn't glammed up today—she wore sneakers and baggy cargo pants, and her hair was stuffed beneath a wide-brimmed straw hat. Instead of neon pink, she was wearing a light blue T-shirt with white numbers on the front.

Kent Grosso, Gina's twin, drove the No. 414 car. His colors were blue and white. Becky was obviously making a statement. Was it confidence, or hope?

Jake wasn't comfortable with either possibility. Nothing he'd learned so far had ruled Becky out as Gina. In fact, the evidence tended to support her claim, but he was a long way from proving anything.

He turned back to Earl. "You've probably seen her picture. She's a model."

"Huh. Guess that explains it. Coulda sworn for a second there that I knew her."

Jake snorted. Apparently, he wasn't the only one who had experienced that phenomenon. "Believe me, I know what you mean. Earl, could you give me the names of some of the guys who worked with Floyd Peters on Shillington's team?"

Earl gave him three names, then launched into a rambling tale of their particular talents and their subsequent employers. Jake jotted down the pertinent bits in his notebook. One of the men was currently with Matheson Racing and should be here today. Though he was grateful for the information, he found himself eager for Earl to finish. Not because he was in a hurry to follow up on the lead. No, he was impatient because he wanted to talk to Becky.

That bothered him. Since when did he let anything take priority over his job? He knew better than to allow his feelings enter into his business. Although Becky Peters wasn't technically his client, she was the subject of his investigation, which was even more of a reason to keep his distance. He couldn't afford to think about her in any way other than professionally.

Uh-huh. And how was that going so far? He'd need a lot more than mental pep talks to get that woman out of his mind.

Jake deliberately kept his gait slow as he worked his way through the crowd toward Becky, giving himself time to observe her. She was talking to a couple who appeared to be in their early sixties, and judging by their body language, good friends of hers. Correction. They were doing most of the talking. Becky's gaze kept straying to the action on the garage floor where the Cargill-Grosso team was readying for the race.

Jake frowned. First the shirt, now this. Was she already assuming she was part of the Grosso family? Great if it was true, but it was going to devastate her if it wasn't. He hadn't been able to forget that flash of lost-child vulnerability he'd seen in her eyes. He'd hate to see her hurt.

She lifted her head suddenly and looked around. Past the handful of people who separated them, her gaze found his immediately. A smile curved her lips and lit her eyes. She looked genuinely pleased to see him.

Well, sure she'd be pleased, he reminded himself before his pulse could speed up any more than it had. He was the guy who was going to find out who she was.

"Mr. McMasters! I didn't expect to see you here."

"There's not much that would keep me away from a race, Miss Peters. I didn't know you were a fan."

The woman she was with spoke up. "Becky grew up watching NASCAR. Hi. I'm Shirley Dalton and this is my husband, Bud."

Jake looked at Shirley and the name she'd given connected. Dalton. They must be Tara's parents. "I'm Jake McMasters."

Shirley raised her eyebrows and gave Becky an inquiring look.

"Mr. McMasters is a friend of a friend," Becky said quickly. "We met last week."

Good, he thought. She couldn't have told them about the investigation yet. He steered the conversation to the upcoming race, which elicited a spirited discussion between the Daltons. Before they could wind down, he caught Becky's gaze and nodded toward the garage exit. "I'd like to talk to you. Could I buy you lunch?"

They left the Daltons in the garage, but not before he got a head-to-toe scrutinizing from Shirley. Becky would have been only fifteen when her mother died. Had Shirley Dalton helped fill the void?

If so, he could understand Shirley's scrutiny of him. She had to be curious why a young, beautiful woman like Becky would want anything to do with a man who was Jake's age and who looked the way he did.

When they reached the infield restaurant, he saw they were in luck. The lineup was short so they only had to wait a few minutes. Their table turned out to be near the kitchen entrance and beside a family with three wriggling kids. Not the quietest spot for a conversation, but it would have to do. Once the waitress had given them their menus and turned to clean up a soda one of the kids had spilled, Jake got down to business.

"Miss Peters," he began.

"Please, call me Becky," she said.

He might as well. He'd been thinking of her that way for days. "Sure, Becky."

"And do you mind if I call you Jake?"

"Whatever you like."

"Thanks." She slipped off her hat and set it on the empty chair beside her. "I've been waiting to hear from you, Jake. You said you'd phone me."

He tried not to be distracted by her hair. He'd known what to expect when she pulled off her hat, yet he took a few seconds to admire it anyway. Even indoors, under artificial light, the color was rich honey, gleaming in lush, inviting waves. His fingers twitched. "I hope you understand that any progress I make has to be reported to my clients first."

"Of course. I'm sorry. I didn't mean to imply you're hiding anything, it's just that…"

"You're anxious for answers," he finished for her.

"Yes!"

"I understand. You mentioned to me before that you've been waiting most of your life to find out who you are."

"Can't you give me a hint of what you've found?"

"Nothing definite yet. I'm working on some leads, but I've spent too many years in this business to make any assumptions before I have proof. That's one of the reasons I wanted to talk to you."

"Yes?"

"I should have mentioned this when we first met. Until I do have proof, I'd appreciate your discretion."

"What do you mean?"

"So far, you're the forty-third woman who has claimed she could be Gina Grosso. It would be too emotionally draining on Dean and Patsy if they allowed themselves to consider each one the real one."

"I see that, but I'm still not sure I get your point."

He gestured toward the numbers on her T-shirt. "For everyone's sake, it would be best not to broadcast the fact that you believe you're Gina."

She sat back as if he'd shoved her. "I'm not broadcasting anything. This is just a shirt, that's all. There are probably thousands like them at the track. Kent has plenty of fans."

"You were hanging around near the Cargill-Grosso garage space."

"What's wrong with that? Do you think I'm some kind of stalker?"

"No. You have no record of that kind of behavior."

"Thanks a lot."

"I meant no offense, Becky. I consider it part of my job to protect my clients."

"Fine. It if helps put your mind at ease, not counting you, the only two people I've spoken with about this are Tara Dalton and Nicole Foster. They're my best friends, and they understand how much this means to me. They wouldn't gossip. I'd trust them with my life."

"Okay. That does ease my mind."

She crossed her arms. Jake suspected the gesture was defensive and wasn't meant as an attempt to cover up the numbers on her chest. He hated having made her feel that way. He wanted to reach across the table and take her hand. Instead, he curled his fingers around the head of his cane. "I'm also concerned about you, Becky."

"Me? Why?"

"I realize that learning your identity is a very personal issue. If you allow yourself to believe you're Gina and it turns out you're not, this could be hard on your emotions, as well."

She drew in her breath as if she were about to make a quick retort, then pressed her lips together and exhaled slowly through her nose. "I know that. I've already told myself the same thing more times than you can imagine."

"Good."

"But in the meantime, I intend to enjoy the possibility."

"Becky…"

"Life would be pretty boring if we didn't take chances, and I'm no coward. What's the point of keeping your heart safe if it means it never gets used?"

He kept his expression impassive, even though he felt as if he'd been the one who had been shoved backward this time.

Yes, he believed in safety, but caution wasn't the same as cowardice. A smart man learned from his mistakes. Jake hadn't risked his heart in almost twenty years, and he didn't intend to. That's why he was so good at his job: he didn't put his faith in anything unless he could prove it. Trust was a trap for the unwary, and love was the bait…

Whoa. Love? Where the heck had that come from? His mind was going way off topic here. He grabbed his menu.

"Is this the reason you asked me to lunch? To make sure I don't stalk or otherwise embarrass your clients?"

No, the real reason I asked you to lunch is because you're a fascinating woman who has haunted my thoughts since we met.

He concentrated on the list of burgers until he was sure the reply that had sprung to his mind remained unspoken. Okay. So he was attracted to her. It didn't have to be a problem. There was nothing wrong with enjoying Becky's company at lunch while he conducted business. This was a good opportunity to learn more—if he tossed a few morsels about his own life into the conversation, she'd be more likely to respond candidly about her own. Once they were done, he would get on with tracking down the leads Earl had given him.

Only this time, he'd make sure he didn't stand around like a pathetic puppy as he watched Becky leave.

He decided to give her one part of the truth. "No, I asked you to lunch because I'm hungry." He smiled crookedly. "And I don't think all that straight on an empty stomach."

BECKY KNEW she was staring but couldn't stop herself. Her brief annoyance with Jake was dissolving as quickly as it had arisen. This was the first time she had seen him smile, and it transformed his face. Even though it was only half a smile, a dimple appeared beside the lines that bracketed his mouth, just as she'd suspected it would. His gaze sparkled, giving her a glimpse of warmth that for some reason he seemed determined to wall up. Why hadn't she noticed how thick his lashes were? They were darker brown than his hair, framing his eyes in a way that turned the light blue into a vibrant, captivating shade.

"What would you like?"

She would like to see a full smile, maybe hear a laugh…

She blinked, realizing the waitress had returned and stood beside their table with her pen poised above her order pad. Becky fumbled for the menu, then asked for a salad and a diet soda. Jake arched one eyebrow at her choice before he ordered a cheeseburger and fries.

"I'm not surprised," he said after the waitress had left. "I had figured models ate nothing but rabbit food."

"How did you know I'm…" She stopped. Of course, he was a detective. He would have easily learned what she did for a living. "Actually, I happen to like salads, but in my business I do have to be careful about my weight. You're lucky that you can eat burgers and stay so, uh, trim."

And *trim* was an inadequate word to describe Jake. He appeared to be in his mid-forties but he showed no sign of excess weight anywhere. He'd rolled his sleeves above his elbows, revealing forearms contoured with lean, ropy muscle. His shirt was pale blue chambray, washed often enough to have softened so the fabric molded his wide shoulders and broad chest. His stomach had the taut flatness that could only come from well-developed abs. The table hid the rest of him, but on the walk to the restaurant she had noticed how nicely his torso had angled into his slim waist and hips. Except for the left leg that he favored, he was in excellent shape.

Becky caught herself before she could begin staring again. Normally, she was as immune to perfect bodies as she was to perfect faces. She'd seen so many of them.

Still, Jake's wasn't perfect. Was that why she found him so interesting?

"I have a high metabolism," he said. "Lucky genes, I guess."

"Sounds like it."

"When I was a kid I was like them," he said, tipping his head toward the children at the neighboring table. Two were standing on their seats while the third was smacking puddles of ketchup on her high chair tray. "I burned off whatever I ate."

Becky watched the kids as the adults at the table tried to regain order, a difficult task for them since they were outnumbered. "Your parents must have had their hands full," she said.

"Yeah. Never realized how hard a job keeping track of kids was until I had to do it."

Her gaze darted to his hands. He didn't wear a wedding ring, yet that didn't necessarily mean he was single. She should have considered that possibility. She couldn't be the only woman to have found Jake so…interesting. "Do you have children, Jake?"

"No, geez, I didn't mean to give you the wrong idea. You're looking at a confirmed bachelor. I meant my little brothers. I had to ride herd on them after our father died and our mom went back to work. They were a challenge."

"That must have been difficult. How old were you?"

"Almost thirteen when it started. But I shouldn't complain." The dimple reappeared in his cheek. "Considering what a brat I had been, taking care of my brothers was justice."

She tipped her head to one side, imagining Jake at thirteen. He must have been a responsible child for his age. Or maybe the circumstances had made him that way. She could readily picture him watching over his little brothers while trying to be the man of the house. He showed signs of having a protective streak now, that was for sure. "It probably helped that you had something to focus on that would keep you busy."

"That's right, you'd know how losing a parent can leave a big hole in your life," he said. "When you lost your mother, you were only a few years older than I was when I lost my father."

"Yes, I was fifteen."

"Is that when you first thought of finding your birth parents?"

"No, it started earlier than that, when I found out I was adopted."

"How did that happen?"

She hesitated. She didn't normally talk about this to anyone, yet if it could help Jake's investigation in any way, she would tell him whatever he wanted to know. "It was on my twelfth birthday," she said. "My parents were having an argument about my party. My mother wanted my dad to stay and help but he needed to work. She used to work at the hospital as a receptionist before I came along but she quit her job in order to take care of me, and so money was tight. It escalated from there to other stuff. They didn't realize I could hear them."

Jake moved his hand on the table. It seemed for a moment as if he were about to reach for her, but he was only picking up his water glass. He took a long sip. "What happened?"

"I heard my father say he had believed adopting a child would have fixed their marriage, but instead I was causing them more arguments."

"I'm sorry, Becky."

I'm sorry, Becky. I didn't see you standing there. Dad didn't mean what he said.

Becky pressed her lips together, remembering her mother's words. She'd forgotten nothing about that day, although she'd tried. Her parents had been almost as upset as she'd been when they realized she'd come back into the kitchen where they'd been arguing. She hadn't wanted to—she preferred to stay as far away as possible during her parents' frequent quarrels. Yet she'd needed some tape to repair a crepe paper streamer that had come loose, and they kept the tape in the kitchen junk drawer. At first her parents had tried to deny what she'd overheard, but their excuses had been transparent, even to a twelve-year-old. Eventually they'd had to admit the truth.

It had been her last birthday party. After that one, she'd never wanted to celebrate her birthday again.

"It's okay," she said finally. "I know they loved me. They just had problems with each other. I did what I could to help."

"Sure, you would have thought their problems were your fault. That's an awful burden for a kid."

His insight was accurate. Learning she had been adopted hadn't been half as hard as learning the reason behind it. She had become increasingly nervous with each of her parents' quarrels. She'd felt it was her responsibility to keep the peace between them, which had been an impossible task, and she'd blamed herself when she'd failed.

"Was that when you decided to look for your birth parents?" he asked gently.

"Yes. It was a childish thing. I fantasized that my real parents were part of a big, loving family and that they had been searching for me for years, not because they thought I'd be useful but because they loved me. I used to build elaborate scenarios in my mind about how they would find me and welcome me back. Then, after my mother died, I felt guilty for wanting to find another mother, as if she hadn't been enough for me. But at the same time, I wanted someone else to belong to more than ever." She laughed self-consciously. "Jake, I don't blame you for thinking I might be stalking the Grossos. All of this sounds a little neurotic, even to me."

This time, when he reached out, he bypassed his glass and touched her hand. "It's not neurotic, Becky, it's natural. I understand why you'd want to be Gina. I just don't want you to get hurt if it turns out you're not."

The contact was brief, only a light graze of his fingertips against the back of her knuckles before he drew back. It left her skin tingling.

Becky returned her gaze to his face. This was like the connection she'd felt when they'd first met, only stronger. Had he felt it, too? Warmth he couldn't quite hide swirled in his eyes, but the rest of his expression gave nothing away. "I appreciate your concern, Jake," she said. "But I need to know the truth, whatever it turns out to be."

"YOU AND YOUR 'friend of a friend' must have had a nice lunch?" Shirley asked, raising her voice over the din of the crowd and the cars as Becky reached her seat.

Becky grabbed her hat to hold it down against a gust of wind. Nice? That was true, it had been surprisingly enjoyable, even though she'd had the feeling that Jake had been subtly pumping her for information.

"Yes, the time flew," Becky replied, realizing that Shirley was still regarding her inquiringly. She waved a greeting at Bud. He smiled but didn't reply—judging by the earphones jammed into his ears, he was more interested in listening to the voices coming over his scanner. "Which team is he listening in on, Shirley?"

"He started out with FastMax and switched to Sanford." Shirley reached into the cooler beneath her feet to pull out a canned soft drink. She offered it to Becky, who shook her head, before she popped the top. "He's still at loose ends now that Dean Grosso retired."

"Isn't he rooting for Kent? Or what about Robert Castillo? Mallory's dating him."

"You know Bud. He doesn't switch his loyalty easily." She gestured toward the tight pack that was entering the backstretch. "Trey Sanford just passed Will Branch. Do you think this could be his year?"

Becky picked out Trey's No. 483 car as it swung around Turn Three. She had dated Trey on and off this past winter. He was a nice man, but neither of them had felt anything special and they had parted as friends by the spring. She wondered now whether she'd dated him because of her inherited affinity for racing…

Jake's caution about assuming she was Gina flickered through her mind, but she blocked it out as the cars entered Turn Four. Trey took it too high, allowing Kent Grosso to nose in front of him. Becky cheered for them both as they swept past.

That was another thing she loved about this sport. It demanded all of her attention. For the next few hours, she didn't have to think about anything else.

THE TELEVISED SPECTACLE was almost as absorbing as being there. Cars rippled across the sixty-four-inch screen in a riot of crayon colors and sponsors' logos. Engines roared, tires screeched and the race commentator's voice boomed from the fourteen speakers that were fastened to the walls. In the center of the floor, three tiers of overstuffed armchairs were arranged in staggered rows so that each provided an unobstructed view. The home theater could accommodate two dozen guests in luxurious comfort, but only one of the chairs was occupied.

Cynthia walked to the middle row and sat beside her father. Though he didn't attend races anymore, he seldom missed the broadcasts. Lit only by the screen, Gerald's face looked as craggy as the acoustic foam that covered the walls. He'd always had a gauntness to his features, but over the past few years his flesh appeared to be drawing in on itself.

He'd seemed invincible when she'd been a child. There had been no request he would deny her, no problem he couldn't solve for her. She'd always been able to count on him. Sometimes she found it hard to believe the father she'd relied on was the same person as this frail old man. When had their roles reversed?

He jerked when he noticed her presence. The controller

he'd left on the arm of his chair dropped to the floor. He doubled over to grope for it, then straightened up and hit the mute. "Did Peters call again?"

Cynthia's ears rang in the sudden silence. "No, Daddy."

"I want to be told immediately if he does. We have to figure out what to do."

She nodded, feeling a stirring of pity as she heard an echo of the man he used to be. Gerald hadn't figured anything out in years. She had found him shaking in panic last week when one of the servants had unthinkingly woken him up to put Floyd Peters's call through to him. She'd fired the idiot the next morning and had left strict instructions with the remaining staff about screening all phone calls through her. "It's all right, Daddy," she said. "I'll take care of it."

"We can't afford to let anyone ask questions about that baby."

"No one will find anything."

"But Peters sounded worried. What if he changes his mind and talks to that private detective?"

"He's kept quiet for three decades. There's no reason for him to go back on his word now."

"I pray he doesn't." Gerald pinched the bridge of his nose, which meant he was trying to think. "We'll be ruined."

We? she thought. No, her father would be fine. In his current state of health, any judge would be lenient when it came to sentencing. Everything Gerald had done, he'd done to help cover up his daughter's crime. Cynthia was the one with the most to lose if the truth got out. In addition to her freedom, there was her position at the company, her reputation in the community, her marriage…

At the thought of her husband, tears started to gather but she forced them back. No. She would not let one youthful mistake ruin a lifetime of achievement. "Daddy, I'm not going to let that happen."

"But—"

"Please, don't get yourself agitated. You know it's not good for you."

"I want to help you, Cynthia, but I don't know how."

"It's my turn to take care of you now, Daddy. The past is going to stay buried. I've taken steps to make sure Jake Mc-Masters doesn't learn anything that could hurt us." She patted his hand, then slipped the controller from his grasp and turned the sound back on. "I have a meeting in a few minutes," she said, raising her voice above the din. "I have to go. Enjoy the race."

He made a weak protest, but his gaze had already moved back to the screen. Within seconds, his shoulders relaxed forward. He looked...relieved.

Cynthia blinked impatiently at another spurt of tears. She truly couldn't rely on her father's help anymore. It was all up to her now.

CHAPTER THREE

"YOU REALIZE those things will kill you."

Jake bit into the hot dog and chewed with gusto, ignoring Len's warning. He'd first met Lieutenant Leonard Denning when the man had been a rookie with the Charlotte police force and Jake had been learning the ropes as a P.I. They'd knocked heads a few times since then, but more often than not they found it mutually beneficial to cooperate. "There's nothing wrong with a nice, juicy hot dog now and then, Len. Pure energy food."

"Do you know what's in them?"

"As long as it's not still moving, I'm not particular." He licked a drop of mustard that was inching out of the bun as he threw a glance at Len's paunch. "Did Nancy get you on a seeds and nuts diet now?"

Len waved a piece of his whole-wheat turkey sandwich. "I'm lucky my wife knows about nutrition and got me to change my habits before it was too late."

"Uh-huh. I heard that too much whole wheat can give you uncontrollable urges to watch the Shopping Channel."

"You know what your trouble is? You need a woman of your own to take care of you."

Naturally, an image of Becky munching on her salad stole into Jake's mind at that comment. "Nope," he mumbled around another bite of hot dog. "Not in the market."

"Hey, Jake." Lurleen, who worked the lunch shift at Edna's

diner on weekdays, paused beside their booth with her carafe in hand. "Do you want a refill on that coffee?"

"Sure. Thanks."

She smiled, brushing his shoulder as she leaned over to pour, then looked at Len. "How are you doing on that milk? Need a refill?"

"No, I'm good."

"Okay, then. Let me know when you're ready for dessert. We've got pecan pie, Jake. Your favorite."

Len watched Lurleen as she moved away, her hips swishing beneath her pink uniform. "I think she likes you."

Jake had been aware of Lurleen's interest for months. She was an attractive woman, but he had no intention of dating her and potentially messing up a good thing. This diner was his favorite place to eat, and he was more concerned about getting food here than getting companionship.

Yet if he did decide to date someone, a woman like Lurleen would be a more sensible choice than a woman like Becky. She was closer to his age. She was good-looking, but not a knockout, so she didn't addle his wits whenever she was around. The memory of her face didn't pop into his mind without warning to distract him the way Becky's had been doing. Lurleen didn't stir up his protective instincts or haunt his thoughts or…

Or interest him in the least.

"Sure, she likes me," Jake said. "I'm a good tipper. You going to eat that pickle?"

"No. Do you realize how much salt is in one of those things?"

Jake plucked the pickle off Len's plate and crunched into it, then slid his plate aside to clear a spot on the table. "Okay, do you have anything else to give me besides tips about better living through fiber?"

Len popped the last of his sandwich into his mouth,

wiped his fingers on a paper napkin and reached into his sport coat. He withdrew a long, buff-colored envelope and tossed it in front of Jake. "Don't laugh. This paper is probably better for you than that hot dog."

"Thanks, Len. I owe you one."

"You bet you do. I've got a tally going."

Jake waited until Len left before he opened the envelope that his friend had given him. Inside was a printout of Peters's arrest record. Jake unfolded the papers and leaned his back into the corner of the booth as he studied them.

He'd been acting on a hunch when he'd decided to pursue the possibility that Floyd Peters was no stranger to the law. There had been something about Floyd's tone, the hint of guilty conscience, that had made Jake wonder how much practice he'd had avoiding questions. His hunch had been right.

There were no recent arrests—all had occurred before he started working with NASCAR. Floyd's first arrest had been at nineteen. Auto theft. The charge had been dismissed after another boy had confessed that he'd done the hot-wiring and Floyd had just been along for the ride.

The next arrest had been for vandalism, but that charge had been dropped, too, without getting to trial for lack of evidence. The third arrest had been more serious. It had been for assault.

Jake shuffled the papers until he found the notes Len had made for him. The assault had taken place at a bar in Charlotte, and had been more of a mutual slugfest than an attack, from the sound of it. Floyd hadn't thrown the first punch, either. He'd been defending himself and his girlfriend from a group of bikers.

Peters had been a hotheaded kid, Jake thought. A little on the wild side, but none of the arrests pointed to a habitual criminal nature. There were no more recent arrests on his sheet after the one for assault, and he didn't actually have a criminal record, since no charges were ever laid. He'd kept his nose clean since he'd married Lizzie, the woman he'd fought to defend.

All right. That fit with the picture of Floyd's character Jake had been putting together. The man had been impulsive and argumentative, but he'd learned self-control. There must have been plenty of passion, both good and bad, in his relationship with his wife. Lizzie must have meant a lot to him, since he'd stood up to a biker gang for her.

The question was, what else would Floyd have done for Lizzie?

There was no doubt their marriage had been rocky. Both Earl and Becky confirmed it. Plenty of couples believed a child would mend a floundering marriage, but the Peters hadn't tried any of the legal adoption routes.

Jake turned back to the copy of Floyd's arrest record. This was the reason Peters and his wife hadn't pursued a conventional adoption. Few legitimate agencies would be inclined to give an infant to a man who had been arrested for assault.

Thus Floyd's options would have been limited. He wouldn't have been able to adopt through an agency, and he wouldn't have the kind of money needed to obtain a child through the unscrupulous, illegal rings who trafficked in babies. It was still possible that he'd known someone who had wanted to give up her child without going through a lawyer.

It was also possible that he'd decided to steal one.

Jake refolded the papers and slipped them back into the envelope as he considered what he knew so far. Floyd Peters had a strong motive to kidnap Gina: he wanted to save his marriage by adopting a child, but he couldn't do it legally. Floyd had opportunity: he had been on the NASCAR circuit the summer the Grosso twins were born, and would have been in Nashville when Gina was kidnapped. Since Lizzie had usually traveled with him, she had likely been in Nashville, too. Both of them would have known Patsy Grosso was pregnant, and both of them would have heard she'd given birth to twins. Had they felt the Grossos could spare one?

Hospital security hadn't been as sophisticated in the seventies as it was now. It wouldn't have been that difficult for the Peters to snatch the baby, since Becky had said that Lizzie used to work as a receptionist in a hospital. Her job would have been in Charlotte, not Nashville, but it would have familiarized her with hospital routines. She could have figured out how to get in and out of a maternity ward without attracting attention. Add to that the fact Floyd had a history of impulsive behavior where Lizzie was concerned and the scenario became not only possible, but plausible.

So, the Peters had means, motive and opportunity. The deeper Jake dug, the more likely it looked that Becky could be Gina. Or…

Or was he interpreting the facts that way because he wanted to make Becky happy?

He groaned and dropped his head into his hands. He couldn't be sure of his objectivity where Becky was concerned. He had seen how important finding her birth family was to her, and from what he'd learned about her childhood, he could understand why. If it turned out that she was Gina, it would be like her youthful fantasy coming true. The Grossos would welcome her with no reservations. She would have someplace to belong. And Patsy would be thrilled to have a daughter like Becky.

So it was absolutely vital for Jake to keep a clear head.

"Here's your pie, Jake." There was the sound of crockery clicking on the table in front of him. "Hey, are you okay?"

Jake didn't recall ordering pie, but Lurleen had brought him a piece, anyway. No, not a piece, a slab. It was so large it hung over the edges of the plate. He thanked her and picked up his fork. The extra sugar was bound to improve the circulation in his brain.

BECKY CHECKED her watch and grimaced at how late she was. It was almost five, so she wouldn't blame Jake if he'd decided not to wait for her. She ran up the remaining flight of stairs to the second floor, then hurried down the hall. Her heart sank when she noticed a man loitering outside Jake's office door.

Jake had told her that he spent most of his time away from his office, which made sense. A private investigator would need to do stakeouts or interview witnesses or follow people. That's what they did in the movies, anyway. There was only so much a person could find out by telephone or computer. She couldn't expect Jake to stay here indefinitely. He had a business to run, and finding Gina Grosso wouldn't be his only case.

"Oh, no," she said as she neared the man by the door. He was short and dark, and though the day's heat had penetrated the hall, he kept his chin against his chest as if he were cold. "Isn't Mr. McMasters there?"

As soon as she spoke, the man shoved his hands into the pockets of his jeans and turned away from Jake's office. He walked past her quickly and headed for the stairs, leaving a whiff of stale cigarette smoke in his wake.

She wondered about the man's behavior for a moment until a high-pitched whine came from the office next to Jake's. It was the unmistakable sound of a dentist's drill.

Becky shook her head in sympathy. The man must have been heading for the dentist, not Jake, and had lost his nerve. She continued to Jake's door. Like the others on this floor, it had an old-fashioned frosted-glass window set into the wood and another window above the lintel. Judging by the lack of an elevator and the worn risers on the wooden stairs, this building was likely as old as her landlady's house.

Jake must enjoy the character of old buildings as much as she did, Becky thought. Otherwise, he probably would have found an office in a place where he didn't have to negotiate a flight of stairs. On the other hand, she couldn't imagine Jake admitting that any obstacle was too much for him.

She tried the knob to find it was locked. Rapping lightly on the door, she tried to peer through the frosted glass but couldn't see any sign of movement inside. Sighing, she stepped back and was about to give up when she noticed the mail slot in the lower part of the door. She was considering whether to leave Jake a note when she heard him call her name.

"Becky!" Jake was walking toward her from the direction of the staircase. "Sorry, I'm late," he said as he approached. "The city decided resurfacing only the roads that weren't one-way would be a good idea. I hope you weren't waiting long."

"Don't apologize. I just got here. We were probably stuck in the same jam." She smiled as he drew nearer. In spite of the cane, his movements were fluid since he incorporated his limp into the rhythm of his stride. He was carrying a dark blue gym bag in his free hand. He must work out, she decided, once again appreciating his trim physique. "Thanks for agreeing to see me."

"No problem." He unlocked his door and ushered her in. "Just give me a few minutes to stash my stuff and I'll be right with you."

The office was deep and narrow, but he'd made the most of the space. A row of filing cabinets lined one wall while a bookshelf and large storage cabinet stood against the other. Farther into the room, two invitingly worn, burgundy leather armchairs were angled in front of a scarred oak desk with a brass banker's lamp. The high-backed chair behind the desk was upholstered in more burgundy leather. Sunlight from the window in the far wall was filtered by a set of wooden-slatted venetian blinds, giving the afternoon a feeling of dusk.

Becky thought the place suited him. The vintage furniture looked comfortable and practical, with no pretenses. All he needed was an outer office with a secretary, a rotary-dial phone and manual typewriter on his desk rather than a computer, and the office could have served as the set for an old detective movie.

Jake took an envelope from his gym bag, unlocked one of the filing cabinets and put the contents of the envelope inside. Next, he took a camera from the bag and placed it on a shelf in the storage cabinet. Becky glimpsed a row of neatly arranged electronic equipment beneath it, along with something that resembled a microphone inside a large, plastic bowl. It must be one of those parabolic microphones like the kind she had seen on the sidelines at football games. This was his surveillance gear, she thought, her curiosity stirring. "Were you on a stakeout?"

"You could call it that."

"What's it like?" she asked.

"Boring. It's a necessary evil in this business, though. Sometimes it's the only way to catch a break."

"Can you tell me about the one today?"

"It doesn't have anything to do with your case."

"That doesn't matter. I'm curious."

He relocked both cabinets, hooked the strap of his gym bag on a wooden coat tree beside the door and looked at her. "Why are you so interested?"

Because you're an interesting man with a darn sexy walk and I want to know more about you.

Becky moved to one of the armchairs and put her purse on the seat. *Sexy* walk? Well, yes, in spite of the limp, it was sexy. Or maybe it was sexy because of the limp. In order to work his cane, he flexed his shoulders and tightened his arm muscles with each stride. For him, walking involved his whole body, and he obviously had excellent control. It must have taken a lot of strength to overcome whatever handicap had caused that hitch in his step. Determination, too. That was more attractive to Becky than perfection. "I've never known a private investigator before," she said. "And look at it this way. If you tell me something about yourself, you can steer the conversation back to me and get more information. You remember. That's what you did when we had lunch."

He blinked, then burst into laughter.

Becky smiled, enjoying the sound. Not many men were confident enough to laugh at themselves, but she should have known that Jake would be. It was a quality that was as attractive as the unique way he moved.

"And here I thought I was being clever," he said.

"You didn't need to be clever. I want your investigation to succeed as much as you do."

"I'll keep that in mind." He walked past her to his desk, turned and leaned back against the front edge. "Okay, speaking hypothetically so I don't break any client confidentiality, if the guy who ran my favorite pizza place was being sued by a customer who slipped on tomato sauce and claimed a bad back, I might stake out the man's house. Then if I got pictures of the customer carrying a ladder and climbing onto his garage roof to reshingle it, the lawsuit would go away."

"Your friend must have been grateful."

"Still speaking hypothetically, he might have promised me free pizza for a year."

"That's great."

"Uh-huh. Pizza's one of the major food groups. Right up there with hamburgers and fries."

She smiled. "How did you get started in the P.I. business?"

"A buddy of mine ran an investigative service and offered me a job when I got out of the military. He retired a few years ago and I took over the business."

"You were in the military? What branch?"

"Army, Special Forces."

Becky could easily picture Jake as a soldier, especially as one of the elite fighters of the Special Forces. He would have looked incredible in a uniform. Now that she thought about it, he still had a certain military pride to his bearing. With his height and impressive physique, he would have been outstanding in combat. Her gaze slid to his leg and her smile faded. "Is that where…" She cleared her throat. "I'm sorry, I shouldn't jump to conclusions."

"No, you're right. That was where I trashed my leg. Operation Desert Storm, to be exact. You would have been in grammar school then." He propped his cane against the desk beside his hip and crossed his arms. "Now it's your turn. Why did you want to see me? Did you think of something else about your adoption?"

She didn't want to change the subject, but she could see by the look on his face he was finished talking about himself. She didn't push. Even though he'd spoken casually about his injury, it was likely a sensitive topic. "No, I didn't remember anything else. I just wanted to let you know I'll be out of town next week."

"Where are you going?"

"I have a catalogue shoot in Rome."

"Georgia?"

"No, Rome, Italy."

"Wow. That's impressive."

"It's not as glamorous as it sounds. I do a lot of catalogue work in Europe. They're always looking for new faces." She dug through the purse that she'd left on the chair. "Here's my agent's number," she said, drawing out a business card. "On the back I've written the number of the foreign agency that booked the shoot. One of them will know the address of the models' apartment."

"Models' apartment?"

"It's usually a condo that's owned by the agency. They rent it to models coming in from out of town. It's a convenient arrangement all around."

He stretched forward and took the card. His fingers brushed hers.

And just like that, her excuse for coming to the office fell apart. It had seemed reasonable when she'd been on her way here, even though she could easily have given him this information over the phone.

Fine, maybe she'd simply wanted to see him. Feel the little tingles when he touched her. Watch the dimple in his cheek deepen with his smile. Hear the calm strength in his voice...

"Thanks."

She pulled back her hand and tucked a strand of hair behind her ear, impatient with herself. Finding her birth family was her priority. Simply because she was developing a crush on the detective who might accomplish that didn't mean she'd forgotten. "It's in case you need to get in touch with me."

"Right. That's good thinking."

"Do you think you might?"

"What?"

"Need to get in touch with me."

Jake slipped the card into his shirt pocket. "Is this your way of asking if I've made progress?"

"Only if you're not going to start into another lecture about not getting my hopes up."

He gestured toward the armchairs, inviting her to sit. "I'm only concerned about you, Becky," he said.

She left her bag on the chair seat and perched on the arm

so her gaze was more or less level with Jake's. "Yes, and I understand you've got a protective nature. You look out for your clients the same way you used to look out for your little brothers. But as much as I used to long for siblings, I don't really need you to be my big brother, Jake."

He recrossed his arms over his chest. "I assure you, Becky, I don't regard you as my sister. And, yes, I've made considerable progress."

"You have? What did you find?"

"At this stage, it's more a matter of what I'm not finding."

"What do you mean?"

"There still is nothing to rule you out as Gina."

She frowned. "Is that what you've been trying to do? Rule me out?"

"It's how I've been investigating all the claimants. It's the quickest way to the truth."

"I would have thought a DNA test would be the quickest way."

He shook his head. "It's not like TV shows, Becky. Thanks to what law enforcement people call the *CSI* Effect, everyone expects science to solve cases rather than old-fashioned detective work, so there are serious backlogs at most analytical laboratories. In real life, unless it's a medical emergency or there's some other way to jump the queue, it can take several weeks to get the results of a DNA test."

"My friend, Nicole Foster, is a doctor. I'm sure she'd help."

"I'll keep that in mind. But besides the wait time, I'd need to get a sample to compare your DNA to, and I don't want to alert the Grossos until I'm more certain."

"How will that happen? I mean, what else do you need to find out about me?"

He considered her question for a while. "Right now, one major issue left to resolve is the exact timing of your adoption. How close was it to Gina's disappearance?"

"I don't know how we can learn that without any records. My dad isn't likely to cooperate."

"I agree with you about your father. I don't believe it would serve any purpose to approach him again at this stage. But I need to find out when you first appeared. It was definitely during the summer of '78. The Grosso twins were born in mid-June."

"My parents always celebrated my birthday on July 7th. That hasn't seemed to bother you."

"No, it doesn't. I'm aware that's the date on your driver's licence, but that doesn't mean it was actually your date of birth. It could have been the date of your adoption, or just a date picked out of the air considering the lack of official information. If you are Gina, then your adoptive parents would have wanted to give you a false birthday to throw people off the track."

Becky felt her pulse skip. *If you are Gina.* This was the first time Jake had used that phrase. It made the possibility more real, somehow.

"But there's a problem," he continued. "If your parents showed up with a baby shortly after Gina disappeared, why hadn't anyone suspected them at the time? The police and the media had publicized the kidnapping. So had the Grosso family. NASCAR had been a small world back then. Someone should have noticed and made the connection."

"Not if my parents didn't show me around."

"Possibly. They could have held off until the heat died down. There was a plane crash shortly after the kidnapping that diverted the media attention…" He snapped his fingers. "That's it."

"What?"

"I heard that your father showed baby pictures of you around the garage."

"That figures. My mother took millions of photographs

when I was a kid. Every birthday and holiday, she'd be running around with the camera and snapping pictures until I saw spots from the flash. But how could that help?"

"For starters, we could get an idea of how old you were when they adopted you. If we're lucky, there'll be some background clue that would narrow down the dates." He pushed away from his desk and grasped her shoulders. "Please, tell me you still have them."

For a second, she couldn't tell him anything. The sensation of his hands on her shoulders was overpowering everything else. His face was so close, she could feel his breath on her chin and could see the blue of his eyes was shot through with tiny flecks of green. Jake really had the most beautiful eyes.

She inhaled unsteadily. It didn't help calm her pulse. Instead, she drew in the clove-and-spices scent of his aftershave and the earthy aroma of warm, male skin. Her gaze dropped to his throat. The top button of his shirt was open. It gaped as he leaned forward, giving her a tantalizing glimpse of his chest. A nice, broad chest, with a sprinkling of dark hair in the center...

"Becky?"

She yanked her attention back to his face. "I only have a few of the albums my mother put together," she said. "My father took most of them with him when he moved to Australia, including all the ones with my baby pictures. But there had to have been more since my mom took so many. I grabbed a few cartons of stuff from the attic when he sold the house. I haven't gone through all of them yet. The extra photographs could be in there."

"Are they at your apartment?"

"Sort of. My landlady lets me store my extra boxes in the loft above her garage."

"How soon does your flight leave?"

"Not until tomorrow evening."

"Great." His gaze dropped to her mouth. "Do you have plans for the morning?"

"Just some packing."

His thumbs moved on her shoulders. It was too light to be a caress. At least, it was light enough so neither of them needed to acknowledge it. "Won't you be spending time with your boyfriend?"

"No. I'm not dating anyone. Why?"

"I'd like to take a look through those photos if you have them, and I'm an early riser. Just wanted to make sure I won't be interrupting anything."

"You won't. How early?"

"How's nine?"

"That's fine. I'm usually up at dawn."

He smiled. "I'll bring breakfast."

Becky could only nod. He wasn't giving her one of his lopsided half smiles. This was a full one, stretching across both sides of his mouth, deepening his dimple, lifting his cheeks and lightening his eyes.

Fortunately, he let go of her shoulders and straightened up before she could do anything stupid. Like lean closer. Or lift her hands to stroke the ropy muscles that flexed in his forearms. Or touch her lips to that intriguing dimple beside his mouth…

Yes, it was a good thing that one of them was keeping their priorities straight.

THE CLEANING CREW had taken their sweet time, and now Ralph Bocci needed a smoke. Bad. He hadn't figured on waiting this long for them to clear out—pushing a broom along the hall and emptying a few garbage cans couldn't be that complicated. They must have been getting paid by the hour, he decided, unwrapping another piece of gum and stuffing it into his mouth. He crumpled the wrapper and was about to toss it on the floor when he thought better and slipped it into the pocket of his jeans instead. As soon as he heard the cleaners leave, he squeezed himself out from beneath the staircase and headed for the second floor.

The dentist's office was tempting—there would be drugs in there that Ralph would be able to sell—but he bypassed it and went right to work on McMasters's door. He hadn't thought it would be any trouble when he'd cased it this afternoon, but it took him longer than it should have to pick the lock. The easiest way to get inside would be to break the window in the door, but Mrs. Brown didn't want the guy to know he'd had a visitor. She was adamant about that detail. No traces.

Ralph chomped hard on his gum to stifle the curse that came to his lips whenever he thought about her. He hated that woman. He should have known better than to have trusted her when she'd offered him a second chance instead of calling the cops. Why should the company brass care what happened to a guy who was caught trying to leave the plant's main parking lot with a car trunk full of cylinder heads? It was obvious now. It was because she'd known about his record when he'd been hired, and now one call from her to his parole officer would put him right back in prison.

Lucky for him, she didn't want him in prison. She wanted him to do her dirty work.

Yeah, real lucky.

Ralph slipped into the office and went straight for the window to close the blinds. He turned on the desk lamp and saw that McMasters had tidied up before he'd left. There was nothing left out except the computer, but that was beyond Ralph's skills. If Mrs. Brown wanted to know what was on it, she'd have to find some tech geek to blackmail. He moved to the filing cabinet next. The lock on it was almost as good as the one on the door. He was nearly out of patience when he felt the distinct *snick* of the lining-up cylinders travel through the lock pick to his fingertips.

Good. It looked like McMasters was old-school. The guy kept notes on paper. Five minutes later, Ralph pulled out the phone he'd been given and pressed the number that had been programmed. A woman answered on the first ring. "Yes?"

"Mrs. Brown?"

"Of course. Don't waste time, Mr. Bocci. Tell me what you found."

Ralph ground his back teeth to hold in another curse, then spread out the file labeled "Becky Peters." By the time he finished reading it to his boss, his mouth was as dry as ash, in spite of the spearmint-flavored gum that was stuck between his molars. He'd heard about the Gina Grosso case on the news a few months ago. Kidnapping was big stuff, even if it was three decades old. Especially when the parents were loaded like the Grossos. He needed that smoke.

"Very good. I take it you remembered to wear gloves."

"Sure," he lied, rubbing his sleeve across the front of the filing cabinet.

"Make certain you leave everything exactly the way you found it and relock the door."

He hated the way she talked. She sounded as if she thought he was an idiot. Too bad she wasn't like her old man. When Gerald Shillington had run the plant, he'd been decent to his employees. He'd treated them fairly. He hadn't made them want to steal from him to make ends meet. "Yes, ma'am. Is that all?"

"Oh, no, Mr. Bocci." Cynthia Shillington Brown's laugh was as irritating as her voice. "We're just getting started."

CHAPTER FOUR

JAKE KNEW he was early, so he parked his car at the curb and took stock of the neighborhood. It was a quiet one, with trees arching over the street and old houses set far back from the sidewalks. Most of the homes had been either restored or well-kept enough not to need restoration. The one where Becky lived was no exception. The two-story Victorian gleamed with a fresh coat of white paint. From what he'd learned when he'd done his initial background check on Becky, the house was owned by a well-off widow who inherited a dry-cleaning chain. She had divided the second floor into two apartments, yet there didn't appear to be an outside staircase. The tenants shared the front entrance with their landlady.

Jake suspected the widow rented the apartments for the company as much as for the income. He liked to think of Becky making her home here. It suited her better than an apartment like his in a high-rise. Living in a family-oriented neighborhood would appeal to her need for roots.

A toddler on a tricycle squealed as he pedaled past on the sidewalk on the other side of the street, followed closely by a yellow Lab that was bigger than the child. A young, heavily pregnant woman hurried after the pair, yelling at the dog and waving a child-size hat at the kid.

Well, early or not, it sounded as if the neighborhood was wide awake. Jake grabbed the paper bag from the passenger seat, got out of the car and headed up the front walk of Becky's house. He was about to climb the steps to the veranda when the inside front door swung open and a tiny, white-haired woman peered at him through the screen door. "Hello."

This must be Becky's landlady, Jake thought, remembering his notes. Lena Krazowski. "Good morning. I'm looking for Miss Peters."

"You must be her friend. She said you were coming. You're early."

Jake was subjected to the same head-to-toe scrutiny that he'd received from Shirley Dalton the previous weekend. "That's right," he said. "Looks like it's going to be a nice day."

"It's going to get hot. Rebecca's in the garage," she said, pointing to the right side of the house.

"Thanks." He pivoted to change direction.

"Mind the delphiniums."

He assumed she meant the flowers that were clustered along the walk. "Will do," he said, giving the bed a wide berth. He followed the driveway to the back of the house, where he found Becky's red compact car and an older-model sedan parked in front of a double garage. Sunshine slanted through the open door, revealing walls hung with an orderly array of gardening tools. An open loft began near the front of the garage and stretched all the way to the back wall. From where he stood he couldn't see anything over the edge except an old brass-bound trunk and several wooden crates. A steep staircase, similar to the kind that folded down to give access to attics, hung from a gap in the center of the loft. He moved toward it. "Becky?"

"I'm up here, Jake." She appeared at the top of the stair-case. "You're early."

"So I've heard." She'd obviously been up there a while. Dust smeared her T-shirt and blue jeans. Her hair was covered with a bright pink kerchief, though a few strands had pulled loose at her temples to dangle in front of her ears. Yet even dusty and disheveled, she managed to look beautiful.

"What's in the bag?"

"Breakfast," he said, holding it up. "I told you I'd bring it."

She shoved a stray lock of hair out of her eyes and glanced behind her. "I'm sorry. I thought I'd find the right box before you got here but they're not labeled."

"Is there space for me up there?"

"Plenty, but it gets hot once the sun gets over the trees."

"With any luck we'll be done by then." He laid his cane on the floor and assessed the staircase. It was steeper than it had appeared at first, more a ladder with wide rungs than a staircase. The wood was old and dried out. It seemed solid enough, but there were some nasty-looking splinters he'd need to avoid. He held the bag between his teeth and grasped the boards at the sides of the risers. Thanks to his workouts at the gym, he could lift a lot more than his body weight. Using mainly his arms, he hauled himself up a few steps until he could grip the edge of the loft and swing himself over it. He got to his feet with the help of a nearby crate, then offered the bag to Becky.

She was staring at him, her cheeks flushed. He couldn't tell whether it was because of heat—the air in the loft was noticeably warmer than down below—or because she was uncomfortable from having witnessed his awkward ascent. He seldom considered himself disabled, but he knew only too well how it could be an issue with some people. He hoped Becky wasn't one of them.

Her eyes lingered on his shoulders. It didn't look like re-vulsion in her eyes. For a moment she seemed to sway toward him, and for an even crazier moment, Jake thought she was about to touch him.

As it turned out, she was only reaching for the bag. "Thanks," she said.

"I hope you like doughnuts."

She opened the bag and looked inside. "This is your idea of breakfast?"

"Hey, I got the kind with fruit. That's nutritious."

"Fruit?"

"I'm pretty sure the gooey red stuff on the inside of the powdered ones has raspberries in it."

"Um, thanks, Jake. That's very thoughtful."

"Anything for another morning person. We're a dying breed."

She wiped the dust from her hands on her jeans, then reached into the bag and drew out one of the covered cups. "I don't suppose either of these is decaf?"

"Sorry. Both are eye-wobbler specials."

"I thought you were a morning person."

"That coffee is why I am."

She pried the top off the cup and passed it to him, then set the bag on top of a nearby trunk. "I appreciate the trouble you went to, but I'm not that hungry."

"There's a fruit plate under the box of doughnuts if you'd prefer that."

"I should have known you were teasing me," she muttered. She grabbed the bag once more, this time taking everything out until she got to the cellophane-wrapped plastic plate. She smiled with pleasure, pulled up a corner of the wrap and popped a strawberry into her mouth. "Thanks, Jake."

"You're welcome. I don't recognize half of what's on there but Lurleen assured me it's edible."

"Who's Lurleen? Your girlfriend?"

"No, she works at my favorite diner. It's been getting in-filtrated by the rabbit food crowd lately so they've had to put some of that fruit and nut stuff on the menu."

She licked a drop of juice from the corner of her mouth. "How tragic."

"Downright insidious." He blew on the coffee she'd handed to him and took a fast swallow. It burned his tongue. Which was good, because it helped him to stop thinking about how delicious the strawberry juice had looked on *her* tongue.

She'd said he'd been teasing, but it had been more. He'd been flirting. Geez, what was wrong with him?

Jake forced himself to look around the loft. The space was larger than he'd expected, and mercifully high enough in the center for him to stand upright. Two more dusty trunks were ranged in the angle beneath the eaves on one side. On the other, sheets of plastic draped what appeared to be several old bicycles and two large-wheeled baby carriages. More plastic sheets covered a group of wicker lawn furniture near the back wall.

His gaze settled on a stack of cardboard boxes on the other side of the packing crate. A few appeared to have been dragged off the top of the pile. He nodded toward them. "Are those yours?"

"Yes." Becky stuffed a large piece of pineapple into her mouth, wiped her fingers on her jeans again and went to kneel beside one of the boxes. "I thought I'd try this one next," she said, ripping the packing tape off the top. "It felt the right weight to have photos."

The first few boxes contained Becky's high-school yearbooks and grade-school artwork. Others were packed with knickknacks and souvenirs from races. The box with the extra photographs turned out to be at the bottom of the stack.

Jake decided she hadn't been exaggerating by much when she'd said her mother had taken a million pictures. Most were still stuffed into the envelopes from the developing company, with the slot for the negatives. Unfortunately, they didn't have the outer envelope with the date the film had been developed, nor had they been packed in any discernible order. The only way to find what they wanted was to look through each one.

By mutual agreement, they settled on the floor with their breakfast and the box of photos between them. This was the kind of tedious detail-checking that Jake was accustomed to doing in the course of his work. Yet after the tenth lot of photos, he realized that he couldn't regard them with the detachment that he should. He was seeing what Becky's life had been like when she'd been a child. She'd appeared healthy and had plenty of toys, but in the vast majority of shots she'd been alone.

He didn't feel pity for her, exactly; it was more of a sadness for what she'd missed. Though it had been annoying at times to share his bedroom and his toys with his brothers, most of the time he'd been grateful for their company. And while his parents had gotten into the occasional argument like any couple, their marriage had been strong. Even after his father had died and times had been tough, Jake had never imagined belonging to any family except the one he had.

Yet growing up alone with battling parents hadn't broken Becky's spirit. She appeared to be a secure and self-confident woman. As she'd told him, she wasn't afraid to take risks with her heart. Patsy was pretty courageous in that regard, too. As for Becky's determination, she might have gotten that from Dean…

If she was Gina, he reminded himself. That was still a big if.

He tucked in the flap to close one envelope and reached into the box for another. The photographs in this one appeared to have been taken when Becky had been around seven, so they weren't any use to him, yet he paused to look at them anyway. He could see hints of the adult Becky in her clear, blue eyes and wide, honest smile. She was holding an Easter basket and wearing a yellow dress that had an embroidered white rabbit, complete with a pom-pom tail, on the skirt. In the next picture, the front of the dress was smeared with what looked like chocolate, as was her smile.

"What?" Becky asked.

He looked up to find her watching him. He lifted his eyebrows. "What do you mean, what?"

"You're smiling. Did you find something?"

He turned the photo around so she could see it. "For a future model, you didn't seem too worried about how you looked on camera."

She laughed. "My mother was always dressing me up for special occasions, but I was happier in jeans. I still am," she added, glancing down at the dirt-smudged denim that covered her legs. She dug into the box for another envelope of photographs. "I'm more interested in whether something's comfortable than whether it's fashionable."

"That's a strange thing for a model to admit."

"Why? Modeling is how I earn my living, that's all. I'm essentially an easel for a client to display his art on. I'm lucky to have a face that photographs well, but that's not really an accomplishment, it's just an accident of genetics."

Jake had no doubt she believed what she said. For a beautiful woman, she had an astounding lack of vanity. "It's more than that, Becky. Your personality comes through in your ads. That's what makes them so memorable." He replaced the photo in its envelope. "How did you get started, anyway?"

"An agent approached me when I was with my friends at a NASCAR race in Richmond. He claimed he could make me a fortune and gave me his business card, but I thought he was a nut." She chuckled and shook her head. "I had just turned seventeen and was taller than everyone in my class, including the boys. I felt like an uncoordinated giraffe. I thought no one would want to pay me just for getting my picture taken."

"What made you change your mind?"

Her expression sobered. She thumbed her stack of photos.

"Becky?"

"It was silly, but remember, I was only seventeen." She set the photos on the floor and looked at him. "As I said, I was taller than nearly everyone I knew, including my father, and I got to thinking about how I must have inherited my height from my real parents. I must have gotten my face from them, too. So I thought that if my face ended up in an ad or on a billboard, maybe they would recognize it and try to find me."

It took all of Jake's willpower to stay where he was. Her eyes held a trace of lost-child sadness again, and he wanted to take that away. Not by finding her birth parents. No, the urge he felt had nothing to do with his case. He wanted to slide across the dusty floor between them, pull her into his arms and kiss her until her smile returned.

He'd come close to doing that yesterday, when they'd been in his office and he'd leaned over her chair. He'd wanted to kiss her then. The feel of her shoulders beneath his hands had gone right to his head. That's why he'd been careful not to touch her today. Didn't seem to make any difference.

Oh, hell. Aside from the whole lack-of-professionalism issue, he was old enough to be her father, a fact these pictures were making crystal clear. He was only a couple of years younger than Patsy and Dean. If they did turn out to be Becky's parents, they wouldn't be too pleased to know she was the object of Jake's middle-aged desire. They would give him the same kind of looks as Shirley Dalton and Lena Krazowski had. And he'd deserve it.

He reached for his coffee, saw he'd already drained the cup, so he grabbed another envelope of photos instead. "It wasn't silly, Becky. Putting the faces of missing children on milk cartons works. It was worth a shot."

"Once I got started, I more or less forgot about it," she said. "It was years before my picture got in anything beyond small catalogues and sales flyers. By then, it was just a job."

"Do you like doing it?"

"Sure. Thanks to my mother's photography habit, I've always been comfortable in front of a camera. Apart from having to keep away from hamburgers and sunshine, I've got no complaints."

"The hamburgers I get, but sunshine?"

"Wrinkles and tan lines."

He remembered the wide-brimmed hats he'd noticed her wearing when she'd been outdoors. "Ah. I'd thought the hats were just a fashion statement."

She smiled. "I do like hats. I've enjoyed the travel, too. The real downside of this business is the lack of job security. I contract for one shoot at a time and can never be sure when my 'look'—" she made quote marks in the air with her fingers "—will go out of demand."

"That's similar to how I work. It's on a case-by-case basis, no security."

"Lucky for you, your detective skills don't have a best-before date. I'll have maybe another three years of steady work and that's it. A lot of clients are finding it's easier to use makeup to transform a twelve-year-old into a twenty-year-old than to make a thirty-year-old woman look younger. Young skin is flawless, and young bodies need less airbrushing. It sets impossible standards for consumers who don't realize to what extent the images they see are being manipulated."

He didn't know anything about the advertising industry so he couldn't dispute what she'd said, but he didn't agree with the reasoning at all. He couldn't imagine not wanting to look at Becky, no matter what age she was. "Have you given any thought to what you'll do afterward?"

She nodded. "I've been keeping up the contacts I've made in the industry and saving my money. I hope to open a clothing store here in Charlotte, something that would be a cross between a fashion boutique and a designer outlet."

It sounded like a doable plan, yet he thought there must be more to it. For a woman who valued family as much as Becky did, and who chose to live in such a family-oriented neighborhood, would she really be content devoting the rest of her life exclusively to a business?

"What's wrong?" she asked. "Don't you think I could pull it off?"

He must be slipping. He hadn't thought she'd be able to read his face. "That's not it. I'm positive you'd be a huge success, but what about getting married and having children? Isn't that something you see in your future?" When she didn't reply, he softened his tone. "A lot of people who grew up with quarreling parents might be soured on the idea of marriage, but I don't think that's the case with you. Given your personality, it's my guess you'd want to establish your own family *because* of your childhood."

She laughed awkwardly. "Wow, you really are a good detective. You have some reasoning skills."

"If you'd rather not talk about it…"

"No, you're right. I confess I'd love to be married with a whole bunch of kids, like the Daltons. You met them at the track last weekend."

"Yes, Bud and Shirley. I remember them."

"My parents' marriage was a bad example. The Daltons showed me how good things could be with the right people. They've been together for forty years and they're still going strong. It would be incredible to have a relationship like that. You'd never have to be alone. You'd always be loved."

It was how he'd already guessed, but it was just as well that she'd spelled it out. He wanted no part of marriage or any of the trappings that went with it, which only added to the list of reasons he shouldn't be having any feelings for Becky. "Yet you're still single. I can't believe it's because you haven't had any offers."

"The short answer is, most guys I date only see this," she said, waving her hand toward her face. She followed that by tapping her finger against the side of her head. "They don't see this. What's your excuse?"

"What?"

"How come you're still single?"

He shrugged. "All that love and marriage stuff holds no appeal for me. I'm not the marrying kind."

"I don't know about that." She pointed at his chest. "I think under all that muscle you've got a soft heart. You care what happens to your clients. You're protective of the Grossos."

"They're family."

"And you wanted to help your friend with the pizza place."

"Sure. We're talking *pizza*."

"You also worry about my feelings."

"I would feel responsible if you got your hopes up for nothing."

She shifted so that she sat cross-legged, braced her hands on her ankles and leaned toward him. "Jake, why are you so determined to deny that you're a nice guy?"

Simple. He knew perfectly well that a relationship between Becky and him couldn't go anywhere, so if he was a nice guy, he wouldn't be ogling her legs, no matter how well her jeans molded her calves and thighs. He wouldn't be noticing how the hollow at the base of her throat was gleaming with dampness from the heat in the loft. And if he had any niceness in him, he wouldn't be wondering what that damp skin would taste like if he placed his lips there and kissed his way up her neck…

Jake gave himself a mental shake. He should get out of here before he made a total ass of himself. He braced his knuckles on the floor, preparing to stand, when his eyes returned to Becky's legs. The photos that she'd set down were fanned out beside her knee. She must have knocked them over when she'd changed position. "Becky, those look like baby pictures."

She followed his gaze, then grabbed one of the photos from the floor. "You're right!" She dug into the box and looked into another envelope. "So are these. Maybe we finally got through to the right layer."

"Great." He pushed himself to his feet. "Would it be okay with you if I took them with me?"

"I thought you wanted to look through them now."

"Changed my mind. It's getting way too hot for me here." He scooped up the envelopes of pictures they'd already gone through and stuffed them into one of the other boxes, then stacked the boxes on the pile she'd taken them from. "Anyway, it's probably better if I continue this on my own."

"Are you sure? It would be faster if I helped."

No, it wouldn't, he thought. Not at the rate he was letting himself get distracted. He closed the flaps of the box with the photos and slid it along the floor to the top of the staircase. "I'll bring this back when I'm done."

She rose and gathered the containers from their breakfast. "All right, if that's what you want."

Not by a long shot, he thought. What he *wanted* was to forget he was working and be seventeen years younger.

Man, he was an idiot. He went down the staircase by the same method he'd used getting up. Becky passed the box down to him, turned around and set her foot on the top step.

Afterward, Jake marveled how quickly it happened. He'd meant to leave, he really had. His intentions had been good. He'd retrieved his cane and tucked the cardboard box under his free arm. Becky was backing down slowly, holding the paper bag from the diner in one hand and grasping the edge of the staircase in the other when somehow, her foot got hooked on a riser. Before she could regain her balance, she went over backward.

Without a thought, Jake dropped both the cane and the box and lunged for her. He felt a sharp pain in his left leg and heard something rip when he collided with the staircase but he managed to steady himself a split second before Becky fell into his arms.

BECKY STRUGGLED to catch her breath. It wasn't like her to be that clumsy. Normally, she didn't have trouble with that staircase but she'd been distracted because she'd been watching Jake and thinking yet again how attractive he looked when he moved and, oh, but his arms were strong. She could feel his muscles flex across her back and beneath her knees and she knew darn well it wasn't the fall that had knocked the air from her lungs.

Yes, *yes*. This was what she'd wanted practically from the moment she'd met him. She didn't care how the embrace had happened, she was just glad that it finally had.

"Are you okay?"

She drew in his scent. It was familiar to her now, that mix of spicy aftershave and male skin. Her eyes half closed in pleasure as more sensations poured over her. He was so solid. Warm, too. Everywhere they touched.

"Becky?"

"Sorry. I must have slipped." Her hands were caught between them. She freed one and flattened her palm against his shirt. Her fingers tingled as she traced the contours of his chest through the fabric. She'd been right about the shape he was in. He was outstanding. Taut and sculpted, tempting her to explore...

What on earth was she doing? She stilled her hand. "Uh, thanks for catching me."

He cleared his throat. "Anytime."

"I'm all right. You can put me down now."

He didn't move to let her go. If anything, he tightened his hold on her.

She gripped his shoulder. "Jake?"

He clenched his jaw so firmly that a muscle jumped in his cheek. "Sure," he murmured. He focused on her mouth. "I need to get going."

Becky could feel Jake's gaze on her lips as if it were a physical touch. She wanted to stay right where she was, but a subtle tremor went through his arms, as if he were straining to hold himself motionless. Belatedly she realized he'd had to drop his cane when he'd caught her. She patted his shoulder. "I'm heavier than I look. You should put me down before—"

"You're perfect, Becky. Absolutely perfect." He paused. "But, yeah, it would be smart to let go of you before there's a problem." He loosened his grip on her legs. The moment her feet touched the floor, he withdrew his arms and grasped the side of the staircase.

A dog started barking from somewhere down the block. A breeze puffed through the open garage door, stirring up the smells of dust and cement. As atmospheres went, it was a far cry from being romantic. Becky tried to concentrate on that rather than the disappointment she felt at the loss of contact with Jake.

The embrace hadn't been deliberate, she reminded herself. He'd just been keeping her from landing on her butt. Even if he'd held her a little longer than he'd needed to, he evidently didn't want to admit it, so she would follow his lead. She brushed off her jeans, giving herself a moment to regain her equilibrium while she looked around for the bag that she'd dropped when she'd fallen. She spotted Jake's cane first and retrieved it. "Here," she said, holding it out to him.

That was when she noticed the rip in his pant leg. She gasped. A narrow flap of fabric had torn free and hung down, exposing his leg from his thigh to his knee. "Jake, what happened?"

He glanced down, then pinched the fabric at the edge of

the rip to pull it aside so he could inspect his leg. "Looks like I caught one of those slivers on the staircase," he said.

"Are you okay?"

"I'm fine." He took the cane from her hand. "It didn't break the skin."

She could see for herself there was no blood on his leg. Most of what was visible through the hole in his pants was scar tissue.

It was the thick, ridged white of an old wound. A horrendous wound. The misshapen tissue encased what was visible of his knee and stretched up his thigh. The full extent of it was hidden beneath the rest of his pant leg, so she could only guess how far down it went. "Oh, my God," she whispered.

"Yeah, it's a sight."

Unable to stop herself, she touched her fingertips to his pant leg beside the rip. She could feel more ridges of scar tissue through the fabric. "This must have been agonizing."

"It doesn't hurt anymore."

She didn't know whether or not to believe that. How could anyone have completely healed from something so extensive? "You said it happened in the first Gulf War. How?"

"It was an accident." He leaned on his cane and shifted back, beyond her reach. "Nothing heroic. A Bradley rolled over on me and some munitions went off."

She dropped her hand. "I'm sorry."

"I'm sorry you had to see it."

"Why? You should be proud of how well you recovered. I can't imagine what you must have gone through to be able to get around as well as you do now."

"Yeah, well, sometimes I forget myself." He moved to the box of photos that he'd dropped. It had landed on its side but was still intact. His shirt pulled tightly across his shoulders as he leaned down to pick it up.

Something had to be wrong with her, Becky thought.

How could she enjoy watching Jake move when she'd just seen the evidence of how much he must have suffered? "I feel stupid for falling."

"Don't worry about it." He tucked the box under one arm and started toward the garage door.

"No, I should have realized moving so fast when you caught me would hurt your leg. I should have gotten back on my feet right away."

He halted abruptly, then set the box on the floor, pivoted with his cane and returned to where she stood. "My leg wasn't the problem, Becky. I was leaning against the steps. I could have held you for another hour."

"I know you're very strong. I didn't mean to offend—"

He shot out his free hand and caught her wrist. "It wasn't my leg that made me let you go, it's the fact I wanted to kiss you."

The frank admission knocked out the air from her lungs. The pleasure she'd felt in his arms returned in a rush, and once again, she had trouble catching her breath.

She tipped her face to meet his gaze. For once, he wasn't masking the warmth there. Honest desire shone from his eyes, sending her heart tripping in response. She didn't try to conceal the effect he was having on her. There was no point. With his fingers on her wrist, he'd be able to feel how her pulse was racing. "I've thought about it, too, Jake."

"That just proves how vulnerable you are because of this case. I don't have that excuse."

"Jake—"

"All this delving into your childhood is stirring up some serious emotions for you. Anybody would get confused. I'd be a real bastard if I took advantage of the situation."

"You wouldn't be taking advantage."

"Come on, Becky. Look at me. I'm forty-eight. I'm old enough to be your father."

"That's irrelevant."

"No, it isn't. You're just getting started on your life. More than half of mine has already gone by. We want completely different things. I shouldn't want to kiss you. I should be looking out for you."

"I'm a big girl, Jake. I don't need you to look out for me."

"Too bad. That's what I'm doing." He rubbed his thumb along the underside of her arm, then released her and held up his palm. "I've got no business having any feelings about you in the first place."

And she shouldn't be having feelings for him, either. She was looking for her birth family, not a man. Jake was right; her emotions were probably confused. She'd already thought of that. This crush she had developed on him might be the result of excitement over what he was doing and gratitude for the fact he was doing it.

Yet none of her reasoning could prevent the effect he had on her senses whenever he touched her. Or stood near her. Or merely looked at her. His cheek was twitching again. Becky lifted her hand and stroked his jaw.

He inhaled hard through his nose. "Becky," he said firmly, "we still need to work together. I'm trying to do the right thing here. You can see that, can't you?"

Yes, she could. She'd felt from the start that Jake was a good man. That was one of the reasons she would welcome a kiss from him. More than welcome it. More than one kiss, too.

Yet he wouldn't kiss her *because* he was a good man.

She drew back her hand, frustrated.

As if that settled the matter, Jake dipped his chin in a curt nod and retrieved the box of photos. Becky watched him go, trying to be grateful for his restraint. But that was tough to do when his walk looked sexier than ever.

CHAPTER FIVE

"DARLING, DO YOU HAVE the sales figures for the last quarter?" Cynthia asked, pausing in the doorway of her husband's office. "The steering arm division in particular."

Hank Brown looked up from the computer and peered at her over the rims of his glasses. "Not yet. When do you need them?"

"By two, if you could." She smoothed her hand over her French twist, ensuring there were no stray hairs. "I've called a meeting with the planning committee."

He returned his attention to the keyboard and poked a few keys with his index fingers. "I'll get right on it."

She murmured her thanks but didn't move away. Even after three decades of marriage, she enjoyed the sight of her husband. He had been blessed with a strong, chiseled bone structure that had only improved with age. The gray hair at his temples gave him a mature elegance, as did the custom-tailored shirts she had ordered for him. He'd draped his suit coat over the back of his chair and loosened his tie, a habit she'd been unable to break him of, yet he still looked handsome enough to take her breath away.

That was how it had been from the moment they'd met. Hank had been driving for the Shillington team then. Cynthia remembered how she hadn't wanted to go to the track that day—she hadn't shared her father's interest in NASCAR—

but she'd had documents that had needed Gerald's signature and so she had driven there straight from the office.

Everything had changed when Hank had squealed his car to a stop and lithely emerged to stand on the pavement. He hadn't won the race, yet everyone had been excited by his top-ten finish. He'd shaken Gerald's hand, then had taken off his helmet and grinned at Cynthia.

His hair had been thick, brown and rebel-long, plastered to his head from the afternoon's heat. His deep-set eyes had sparkled with race-fueled adrenaline that hadn't yet faded from his system. He'd been tall and lean, his body humming with excitement as the sleek, powerful machine he'd managed to control for hundreds of laps had steamed behind him.

In that instant, Cynthia had been struck with a wave of longing unlike anything she'd known before. She'd wanted Hank. It didn't matter that he was younger than her, or that he was merely her father's employee. She'd been crazy with the urge to possess him and had been unable to think of anything else. She'd joined Gerald on the NASCAR circuit, taking advantage of any opportunity that would get her close to Hank. She would have done anything to make him love her…

"Is there something else you wanted, Cynthia?"

She put on a smile. "No, darling. I'm simply admiring how handsome you look this morning."

His jaw tightened. "I need to get to work on those figures you asked for," he said.

She lifted her hand in a parting wave and returned to her office. Hank had appeared tense. She'd have to look into getting an assistant for him. He'd been given several different positions at Shillington Enterprises during the years after he'd quit racing. She'd thought he was happy in his current placement in the accounting department—he'd shown an unexpected aptitude for numbers despite his lack of higher education—but perhaps he was overworked.

Her steps faltered. There was another possibility for his tension. Hank might be sensing her own worry over the problem with the girl. He'd probably noticed that Gerald had been more agitated than usual lately, too. She'd done her best to maintain the regular routine at home, but it was difficult to shoulder this responsibility alone. She would have to try harder, for Hank's sake. It was because of him that she'd taken that baby in the first place. It had seemed so long ago…before this life she'd built for him. She'd wanted so badly to win his love.

Cynthia closed her office door, leaned back against it and pinched the bridge of her nose. It was the same gesture she'd seen her father make a thousand times when he tried to think. Yet Cynthia had difficulty concentrating through the emotions that clouded her mind. Hank was hers. Fate had bound them together even before they'd exchanged their wedding vows. After everything she'd done for him, she couldn't conceive of losing him.

But she knew, with the instinct of a woman in love, that Hank would never forgive her if she told him the truth. He had a simplified concept of right and wrong, a holdover from his blue-collar roots. He wouldn't care what a scandal would do to the company the way she did. Sometimes she suspected he didn't care about their marriage as much as she did, either.

No! She wouldn't go there. The counseling had done wonders. She and Hank were happy. She would ease his workload, perhaps arrange a vacation for the two of them once this was over. Then everything would be fine, just the way it had been before.

Squaring her shoulders, she pushed away from the door, took out her cell phone and called Ralph Bocci.

He answered after seven rings. His voice was thick, as if he'd just awoken.

Cynthia glanced at her watch and scowled. "What have you learned?"

"What? Oh, yeah. Hang on." He cleared his throat, then started to cough.

It was a phlegmy, disgusting sound. She held the phone away from her ear until he finished. "You should use a nicotine patch, Mr. Bocci."

"Sure. I'll get right on that." There was the click of a lighter, followed by a soft squeak as he drew on his cigarette. "The girl's in Italy for a week."

"Why?"

"Some modeling contract. You want her agent's number?"

What use would that be? Bocci was an idiot, Cynthia thought. She hadn't had much choice, though. She couldn't very well have interviewed candidates for the job she'd given him. She strove to retain her patience. "That won't be necessary. What did you learn about the investigation?"

"There was nothing new in the files. Seems to me the investigation is stalled. With the girl out of town, looks like McMasters is taking a break."

"That's no excuse for you to do the same, Mr. Bocci."

"I never said I was."

Cynthia wanted to believe him, just as she wanted to believe that the detective was slowing down. With stakes this high, though, she couldn't afford to do either. "Spare me the protestations of innocence," she snapped. "Both I and your parole officer know exactly what kind of character you possess, so unless you want me to enlighten him about the material you tried to steal from my company, you'll go and do what I tell you."

JAKE PULLED into the lot at the Halesboro track and shut off the ignition. The smell of rubber and exhaust, along with the whining buzz of racing engines, came through the open window. Since it wasn't a NASCAR-sanctioned track, the Cargill-Grosso team was testing here today, so it was a good opportunity to catch up with the person he needed to see. Casually, though. He wanted to keep this low-key, for everyone's sake. That should be easy to do, since he was family and he followed the team closely enough that no one would think his presence at the track was unusual. All he had to do was get a handle on the anticipation that was curling through his gut.

He took a deep breath, then reached into his shirt pocket for the snapshot that had brought him here. The baby in it appeared too young to lift her head, so she would have been only a few weeks old. She was strapped into a plastic infant seat that had been set on the middle of a round, wooden table. The picture had been taken in the Peters's kitchen—the yellow cabinets and the seventies-style flowered wallpaper in the background looked the same as they did in pictures where Becky was older. There was a white rectangle on the wall in the upper right corner that was probably a calendar, but it was too blurry to show any details.

It didn't need to. The date was obvious. The baby was dressed in a red, white and blue sleeper that was adorned with tiny stars. Floyd Peters was leaning across the table, a sappy grin on his face while he waved a miniature flag on a stick to amuse his new daughter.

There had been almost two dozen other pictures in the envelope where he'd found this particular shot. They presented a record of what must have been one of Becky's first outings. Becky had cried. She'd had a bottle. She'd gone to sleep in a baby stroller with her bottle tucked beside her. She'd nestled in Floyd's arms while he'd stood on the sidewalk to watch a parade go by.

A Fourth of July parade.

Unless Peters had invented a time travel machine, Becky's birthday wasn't the seventh of July.

Her parents had lied. They hadn't been very good at it, either, since they'd taken their own photographic evidence that would prove they'd lied. They'd obviously thought better of it afterward, though. That's why these pictures had never made it into a photo album. They'd been crammed into the bottom of a box, stuck in an attic and forgotten about. It would have been smarter to destroy them, but the Peters had doted on their new baby. They wouldn't have wanted to lose the memories they'd captured on film.

Jake tapped the photo against his palm. It still wasn't proof that Becky was Gina. There could have been some other reason the Peters had wanted to conceal their daughter's actual birth date.

Yet the facts continued to point in that direction. Jake knew what a newborn looked like. His sisters-in-law had been producing children on a regular basis, and they'd been almost as camera-happy as Lizzie Peters. His nieces and nephews had all shared that same wide-eyed, somewhat startled look when they tried to focus on things, and they all had the same floppy, neckless body shape. It was a safe bet that Becky had been born around the same time as the Grossos' missing baby.

When he'd found this picture three days ago, his first impulse had been to call her. She'd been gone since the weekend and he'd already been missing the sound of her voice. He knew she'd be thrilled with the news. He could imagine how her tone would rise with excitement. She'd probably laugh when he described the picture to her and then make some comment about how her mother had liked to dress her funny. He liked the sound of her laugh. He wanted to make her happy.

Yeah, right. He wanted a lot more than that.

Which is why he hadn't called her. It was just as well that Becky was currently on the other side of the world. Distance was exactly what they both needed.

Jake slipped the photo back into his shirt pocket, got out of his car and headed for the track. The drivers were giving each other some friendly competition, in spite of the fact it wasn't a race. Jake watched while they sped across the back-stretch, then he scanned the infield, looking for Dean. The team was doing well this season, thanks in large part to Dean Grosso's steady guidance.

The family had had a lot to deal with, starting with the murder of Alan Cargill just before the ownership was to be transferred to the Grossos. More than seven months had passed since then with no charges being laid, yet the New York cop who was working on the case, Lucas Haines, had struck Jake as a competent man, so he had faith that the culprit would be found eventually. It had been tough on the Grossos to lose their friend in such a violent way. They'd only begun to come to terms with it when the news that Gina might still be alive had broken.

Dean and especially Patsy had taken it hard. They'd mourned their daughter years ago, and ripping open that old wound must have been painful. Jake would be only too glad to bring the Grossos some good news, but there was no way he would set them up for more heartache.

He spotted Dean standing beside the starter's tower. His thick, brown hair and broad shoulders made him easy to pick out, but what really distinguished him was his body language. He looked like a man accustomed to being in charge, whether it was behind the wheel, as he used to be, or behind the team as he was now. He didn't look like Becky, but as Jake had thought before, the two did share a certain stubbornness. At the moment, Dean appeared deep in conversation with his crew chief. Jake took advantage of that and headed in the opposite direction.

The No. 414 car pulled into the pits trailing a puff of blue smoke. Kent Grosso emerged and yanked off his helmet as he gestured toward the hood. By the time Jake neared, the pit crew had already surrounded the car and were working to make adjustments. "How's it look, Kent?" he called.

Kent glanced toward him. "Hi, Jake. Didn't know you were coming."

"Yeah, I had the afternoon free so I thought I'd drop by."

He nodded, his attention still on the car. Kent focused the way Dean did, his posture radiating the same kind of confidence. He'd inherited his Italian features from his father's side of the family, with the exception of his blue eyes. They were a striking shade that was more intense than Becky's. Still, his height and body type were more similar to Becky's than to his parents'.

As a matter of fact, Kent was exactly the same height as Jake, but that similarity was probably due to coincidence, not heredity. Jake was Patsy's cousin several times removed. The blood tie between them had happened generations ago.

That was good. If Becky did turn out to be Gina, her kinship with Jake would be distant enough that there wouldn't be any medical reason why they couldn't—

Jake slammed the door on that thought before it could finish forming.

"It's nothing serious," Kent said. "The engine's just got the usual prerace hiccups."

"I heard it's going to be a hot one this weekend. The forecast for Chicago's calling for high nineties."

"That's what we figured." Kent stepped back to give one of the mechanics more room. "Are you coming to the barbecue after the race?"

"Wouldn't miss it." Jake leaned closer and pitched his

voice so only Kent would hear him. "Can you spare a few minutes? I need to run something past you in private."

Kent lifted his eyebrows at that, but didn't question Jake's request. He left his helmet in the car and followed him to a picnic table in the shade of the garage. "I have to put in some more laps," he began.

"That's fine," Jake said. "I'll be quick. I'd like you to provide a DNA sample."

"A DNA… This is about Gina."

"Yes."

"Don't tell me you found her!"

"It's a strong possibility."

"Who is she? Where is she?"

"The woman I'm currently investigating is Becky Peters," he said, pulling the photo from his pocket. "This is her in '78. I won't go into all the details now, but I think it's worth doing the test."

"Sure. Of course. I'll do whatever you need." He peered at the picture. "Cute kid."

"That's nothing. You should see her now."

"This is incredible. That baby could be my twin. Mom and Dad are going to be—"

"Hold on, Kent. I don't want to tell them yet. That's why I asked you for the sample instead of your parents. As Gina's twin, your DNA should provide a good basis for a match." He returned the photo to his pocket. "I don't want to get Dean and Patsy excited and then have it turn out to be a false alarm. Your mother concerns me the most. If Patsy got her hopes up and the test showed no match, it would be like losing Gina twice."

"I understand." He looked toward the tower where his father was still talking with the crew chief. "Dad's trying to be the strong one about all this, but I know he's anxious, too. He blames himself for not looking harder after Gina disappeared."

"He shouldn't. The police told him Gina was dead. They had to move on. It was the only healthy thing to do."

He regarded Jake once more. "I'm glad you came to me, Jake. I want to find my twin as much as everyone else, but I never even knew she existed until a few months ago. If the test shows no match, it's not going to hit me like it would my parents."

"Thanks, Kent. I'll make the arrangements and get back to you."

"Great." Kent gave him a thumbs-up as he returned to his car. Minutes later, he was back on the track and roaring through the first turn.

Jake remained at the picnic table to watch the action. Like the cars hurtling past, the events he'd just set into motion would be hard to stop. Was he jumping the gun with the DNA test? Possibly. Last week he'd told Becky he'd wanted to be more certain before he took the final step, but that had been before he'd felt her in his arms.

He clenched his jaw as the memory flooded over him. He couldn't understand why he kept thinking about it. He'd held plenty of women, and in far more intimate circumstances. Why had one fully clothed encounter in a dusty garage made such an impact? And why the hell had he decided to talk to her about it?

He shouldn't have brought the attraction into the open. He'd done a good job of keeping his feelings to himself until then, but his pride had gotten the better of him. He hadn't wanted a young, beautiful woman like Becky to believe his bum leg had been the reason he'd cut short their embrace.

So instead of simply walking away, he'd told her he'd wanted to kiss her. Uh-huh. That had been so much smarter.

Which only went to prove that Jake couldn't rely on his judgment with anything concerning Becky anymore. Luckily, DNA wasn't a matter of judgment, it was science.

"WE DO IT once more. I do not like the shadow." The photographer barked instructions in Italian to his assistants, who scurried to adjust the reflectors at the edge of the set. The shoot was taking place in a studio rather than outdoors, which allowed more control of the lighting and more efficient clothing changes. It also meant less opportunity to move around. Becky used the delay to straighten up and stretch the ache out of her back.

"Tired, *bella?*"

She glanced at the model beside her. "I don't have any complaints, Paulo."

"I do not, either. It has been purely pleasure working with you."

Somehow she restrained herself from rolling her eyes. Paulo had been coming on to her all afternoon. She suspected it was mainly to relieve the boredom between shots.

"You are too warm, *cara.* Permit me to help before the maestro notices the dampness." He pursed his lips and curled forward to blow lightly on her skin above her bikini top.

Becky leaned back. "Give it a rest, Paulo."

"I only want to dry your skin. We do not want more delays while makeup is called."

"Well, thank you. That's a wonderfully selfless gesture. But in case it escaped your attention, we're modeling swimwear. We're supposed to be damp."

He smiled, showing her his perfect teeth. Even amid the collection of perfect bodies and faces that had been assembled for this project, he was startlingly good-looking: dark, brooding eyes, sharply defined features and thick, black hair that was slicked boldly back from his forehead. He gestured to the six-pack abs that graced his torso. "Perhaps you could help me, as well. These lights make me hot but your hands are cool. If you could rub me here…"

"You're original, I'll give you that."

"What else will you give me, *bella?*"

"Advice. You're wasting your time."

"No time with you could be wasted."

"Does that Latin lover act actually work on anyone, Paulo?"

"It does." He winked. "I will be happy to provide references if you wish."

She bit her lip. She didn't want to laugh or it would only encourage him. She was saved from having to respond by the art director, who used a mangled mixture of languages to order everyone back into position.

Paulo immediately slipped his arm behind her waist and propped his chin on her shoulder. She smiled for the camera. The pose was tame and not suggestive in the least. It was meant to display the swimwear in an atmosphere of friendliness and fun. Becky suspected there was a grain of truth in Paulo's bragging, because there likely were plenty of women who would enjoy having his spectacular body so close to theirs.

Yet the contact did nothing for her. No tingles, no shivers of awareness, nothing other than mild irritation with the way the fashionably macho beard stubble on Paulo's chin was abrading her skin.

Now, if it had been Jake standing next to her like this, practically naked and breathing on her neck…

Oh, yes, that would definitely do something for her. She could only too clearly imagine what the sculpted muscles that she'd felt through his sleeves would feel like against her skin. She didn't think it would bother her to feel his beard stubble against her neck, either. Even better, what if it was first-thing-in-the-morning stubble and he was waking her up with a nuzzling kiss?

She inhaled unsteadily, surprised by the rush of heat. She'd thought that distance would give her some perspective. Everything Jake had said about her being emotional and vulnerable had been right. A crush should have faded, especially now that she was immersed in her work. She needed all the contracts she could get if she was going to boost her savings. Although the investments she'd chosen had been performing beyond her expectations lately, she still needed more before she could open her own business.

Yet from the time she'd arrived in Italy, all she could think about was how soon she could go home.

"NICOLE! What are you doing here?"

"Waiting for you. How was your flight?"

"Completely ordinary," Becky said, still trying to absorb the fact Dr. Nicole Foster was at Charlotte-Douglas International Airport. She'd been friends with Nicole almost as long as she'd been friends with Tara, but neither one had ever met her at the airport after one of her modeling jobs. Why would they? Becky's trips were routine.

She peered at her friend more closely. Nicole looked well. More than well. She looked fabulous, as usual. Becky had always admired her combination of red hair and blue eyes, characteristics that were made all the more striking by the energy that simmered beneath the surface. Yet was that a hint of tension around her mouth? "Nicole, is something wrong?"

"Relax, everything's fine. Where's your luggage?"

Becky tipped her head toward the carry-on bag that hung from her shoulder. She'd learned to travel light when she was working—most of the time she wore clothes provided by the client and the rest of the time she preferred easy-care, packable knits. "This is it."

"Great," she said. She checked her watch, then turned and started walking. "Let's get out of here."

Becky followed on her heels as they worked their way through the crowd. "Nicole, it's really nice of you to meet me like this. Don't get me wrong. It's always great to see

you, but I don't remember even telling you which flight I'd
be on."

"You didn't. Jake McMasters did."

"Jake?" She looked around quickly, half expecting—no,
half hoping—to see him. "Why would he—" She halted, her
hand going to her mouth. "Oh, God. Is he all right? Did
something happen?"

"Will you relax?" Nicole caught her arm and urged her
to start moving again. "He's fine. It's interesting that you'd
be so worried about him, though. Why is that?"

"I... Don't change the subject. Why are you here?"

"I'll fill you in when we get to my car."

It wasn't until they had left the lot and joined the afternoon traffic on the parkway to the city that Nicole finally
could devote her attention to Becky's questions. "Jake called
me a few days ago," she said. "He told me that you gave
him my name."

"What? I don't remember..." Becky thought about it.
She had indeed mentioned Nicole to Jake. The man must
have an exceptional memory. "Oh, right. Well, that explains
how he knew who you were but not why you're here. Are
you deliberately dragging this out and acting mysterious
just to make me crazy?"

Nicole grinned and gave her a sideways glance. "You
know me too well."

"Nicole," Becky said, twisting on the seat to face her. "I'm
hungry and I'm jet-lagged and used up my quota of patience
on a certain overly amorous hunk of walking ego, so—"

"Ooo, that sounds delicious. Who was he?"

"His name was Paulo but don't change the subject. Need
I remind you that I'm bigger than you?"

She laughed. "Not by much."

"Nicole..."

"All right, all right. Jake called me because you already

volunteered my help as a doctor. He wants me to take some DNA samples."

It took her a few seconds to process what she'd heard. She dropped her head against the headrest, stunned. "Jake wants a DNA test to see if I'm Gina."

"Yes."

Her mind was spinning. "This is so fast. When I left he was still being cautious about it. He said he didn't want to have the test done until he was more certain."

"Oh, he's still being cautious. He tried to play it down."

"What do you mean?"

"When we first met at my office, we got to talking about how I do weekend work at NASCAR races and I mentioned that my father was an itinerant doctor in Tennessee. You know, how my dad took jobs filling in for other doctors while they were on sabbatical or vacation?"

"Sure, I remember. You talked about that when the story of Gina's kidnapping broke."

"Well, Jake pointed out that my father could have been working at the hospital in Nashville when the Grosso twins were born. I'm the right age, too. He said for all we know, *I* could be Gina."

Becky did her best to squash the resentment she felt. She knew that until they had proof, Jake would have to continue considering every possibility. That was what the Grossos had hired him for. He had every right to look at another woman as a potential Gina. That didn't mean he was being disloyal to Becky, it meant he was doing his job. He'd made it perfectly clear before she'd left that their relationship would remain professional.

"Not that I am," Nicole said.

"What?"

"Gina. That's reaching. You look a lot more like the

Grossos than I do. I look like my father. Anyway, I think Jake was going out of his way to demonstrate he's still keeping an open mind. If you ask me, I'd say he's concerned about you getting your hopes up."

Becky sighed. "That sounds like Jake, all right. He takes caution to a whole different level."

Nicole took her hand from the wheel and squeezed Becky's knee, then flipped on her signal and steered toward the exit. "I'm concerned, too. I know how important finding your birth family has always been to you. At the same time, I've been so excited to be part of this, it's been hard waiting for you to get home."

"Thanks, Nicole." She took note of the exit they were heading for. "I take it we're going straight to your office now."

"It was the only time we could arrange that worked with everyone's schedules. Do you mind?"

Becky assured her that she didn't. In a way, she was glad that Jake hadn't warned her earlier, because by the time they pulled into the parking lot of the clinic where Nicole worked during the week, Becky was already feeling too antsy to wait. They went through the rear entrance of the building and down a short hall to Nicole's office.

Jake was already there. He rose from his chair when they entered the room, his gaze meeting Becky's. He smiled. "Welcome back."

A week apart hadn't made any difference, Becky realized. Nor had being around some of the world's most beautiful people. Jake's crooked smile, his finger-combed hair and his plain, faded chambray shirt looked so good, so familiar, she wanted to walk straight into his arms.

But then the man who had been sitting in the chair beside Jake's got to his feet and turned to look at her.

Becky didn't need an introduction—she recognized him instantly. Kent Grosso's face was well-known to every NASCAR fan. Yet he wasn't here because of what he did for a living. He was here because he could be her twin brother.

That's when the significance of what was happening hit Becky full force. After so many years of dreaming about it, she could finally be meeting a member of her family. She barely heard what Nicole was saying. Instead, she moved toward Kent and extended her hand.

He clasped it immediately, studying her as openly as she was studying him. "You're almost as tall as me," he said. "And your hair's nearly the same color as our mother's… I mean, if you're…" He smiled. "Does this feel as weird to you as it does to me?"

She laughed. "Yes! I don't know what I should say to you. Other than thanks for agreeing to the test."

"It's no trouble. They promised it would be painless."

"That's right," Nicole said, snapping on a pair of gloves. She peeled paper wrapping from a long swab and gestured to Kent. "All you need to do is say 'ah.'"

Nicole swabbed the inside of Kent's cheek, placed the sample in a plastic vial and sealed it, then repeated the process with Becky. She inserted both vials in a padded envelope that she took from her desk, added a sheaf of paperwork and sealed the flap.

For something that could have a profound impact on Becky's life, the procedure had seemed far too simple.

"I'll drop this off at the lab on my way home," Nicole said, looking at Jake. She handed him a thin sheet of yellow paper. "Here's your copy of the test form."

"Thanks. I appreciate your help, Nicole," Jake said. "And your discretion."

She smiled at all three of them. "It was my pleasure."

"When do you think we'll get the results?" Kent asked.

"I've asked the lab to give it priority," Nicole replied. "But I can't promise anything. It could be weeks before they get around to it."

Kent looked at Jake. "So, what do we do now?"

"There's nothing much we can do except wait for the scientists to do their job," he said. "My part in this is over."

And that's when the rest of what was happening hit Becky. The DNA test was the final step in Jake's investigation. There would be no point for him to investigate her further. If the results showed she wasn't a match with Kent, Jake would move on to the next Gina claimant. If it did show a match, he could close his case. Either way, their association would end.

"Becky?" Jake asked. "Are you all right?"

She forced a smile. "Sure, just jet-lagged."

This should be one of the happiest moments of her life, Becky told herself. She could be on the road to joining the family of her dreams. That was what she wanted, wasn't it?

Well, wasn't it?

CHAPTER SIX

"ALL RIGHT," Becky shouted, pumping her fist in the air. "That's how you do it. Go, Kent!"

Jake added his voice to the cheer that went up from the group around them as Kent nosed into the lead. He held it for three laps, although Zack Matheson remained on his tail, vying for an opening that Kent was too savvy to give him. Kent and Zack had just flashed past again when the crowd gave a collective gasp. Somebody farther back in the pack blew a tire in a puff of smoke. The caution flag came out. While the drivers throttled back and held their positions, the Chicago track crews scurried to pick up the debris.

Becky took advantage of the drop in the level of engine noise to speak without having to shout. From their vantage point near the entrance to pit road they had a great view of Turn Four and the straightaway, but it brought them close enough to feel the vibrations of the engines through the soles of their feet. "What's that?" she asked. "The sixth caution?"

"Seventh," Jake said. "I figured it would be bad in this heat. Are you okay? You want to find some shade?"

She tipped the brim of her hat to shield her face from the sun and craned her neck to keep track of Kent's car. "Maybe later. I love being this close to the action. It was really nice of Kent to arrange a hot pass for me."

Before they had left Nicole's office the other day, Kent

had offered to obtain an infield credential for Becky for this race. Jake had been concerned there would be questions from the Grossos about who she was that would be difficult to answer. But after one look at the pleasure on her face from Kent's offer, he hadn't had the heart to object. As it turned out, he'd worried for nothing. They'd simply told anyone who asked that Becky was Jake's friend.

It wasn't really a lie. Jake did like Becky. He enjoyed her company. That he also desired her would be a big complication to a potential friendship, but it was one he should be able to manage.

Sure. He'd be fine as long as he concentrated on the smell of burnt rubber instead of the delicate hint of gardenias that rose from her skin. No problem, as long as he ignored the feel of her arm brushing against his or their hips bumping as they shifted to follow the action on the track.

Why had he thought that time apart would have dulled his reaction to her? "Yeah," Jake said. "Kent's a decent guy."

She tapped her fingernail at the card in the plastic holder that hung on a lanyard from Jake's neck. His pass was good for the season, not just one race like Becky's. "You've got no idea how lucky you are, being related to Patsy," she said. "You get to do this all the time."

"The credential isn't only because I'm family, it's because of the case Dean and Patsy hired me for. Right from the start that anonymous blogger claimed Gina was close to NASCAR. Racetracks are good places to gather information, so the Grossos made sure I'd have full access."

"I've followed NASCAR all my life. That's another point about me that fits with Gina."

"Along with most of the crowd in the stands."

Her finger stiffened against his chest. "Don't start on that again, okay? I don't want to have to hit you."

He lifted one eyebrow. "Hit me?"

"I got your message loud and clear weeks ago. I'm not assuming anything about being a Grosso. I know nothing's certain until the test results come through. I'm just making the most of the circumstances."

"You're hoping, though."

"Well, of course, I'm hoping. That's the only reason I came to you in the first place. Now that you found those Fourth of July pictures of me, I've got even more reason to hope."

"I'll return that box of photos to you when we get back to Charlotte. We could swing by my office on the way from the airport if you like. It won't be much of a detour."

"Thanks, Jake. I'd like to see them, considering how important they might turn out to be. It's funny, though."

"What is? The pictures? Not more than a lot of the others I saw in that box."

"No, not the way my mother dressed me. I mean the fact it was a photograph that tipped the scales for you with this investigation. Sometimes it seems I've lived my whole life through a camera. It's as if part of me only exists in pictures. It's just…strange."

"Is this about your job? I thought you liked modeling."

"Sure, but all along it's only been a means to an end. I started it because I wanted to find my family." She laughed softly. "It's kind of ironic that it could be a photograph that *does* bring me my family in the end."

"Becky…"

"Don't say it, Jake." A lock of hair slid out from beneath her hat brim to dangle beside her eye. She blew it aside. "You know, too many cautions in a race can get tiresome after a while."

"Maybe, but they're the only way to clear the track to make sure no one gets hurt."

"That's just it. At some point, the action has to be allowed to get going again."

"Unless you're driving, the action's out of your control."

"So, to stretch this metaphor even further, who's driving? You?"

"The lab techs. My job's over."

She parted her lips as if she was about to make another retort, then paused to study his face. "That's right. Unless the test results show no match, your job's over."

"Right."

"Then why are you here?"

He gestured toward the conga line of cars that was passing in front of them. "I'm watching the race."

"No, I mean why are you here with me?"

"You know why. It's so no one questions why Kent got you a pass."

"That's a pretty thin excuse, Jake. You know what I think?"

"What?"

She spread her fingers over his chest and leaned toward him. "I think it's because you missed me last week as much as I missed you."

Smart woman, he thought.

This was where he should lie. Tell her that he hadn't thought of her at all except in his capacity as an investigator. Do the noble thing and distance himself so he didn't take advantage of her vulnerability. Claim that his heart hadn't leaped at his first sight of her and pretend that her gentle touch on his chest wasn't doubling his pulse rate.

She held his gaze, waiting for a reply.

Despite his best intentions, the lie wouldn't come.

"Hey, Becky!"

Becky dropped her hand and turned toward the voice. A young, dark-haired woman waved as she approached from one of the other haulers. Becky waved back. "Hi, Sarah! How are you doing?"

"Great." The woman smiled a greeting as Becky introduced her to Jake as Sarah Reynolds. "This is some season so far, isn't it?"

"That's for sure. No shortage of excitement."

Sarah glanced around. "So you've finally gone over to the enemy."

Becky laughed. "You know me. I've always rooted for the driver who's the most fun to watch."

"That's why they keep me hopping," Sarah said, moving away. "My job is never done."

Becky waited until the woman was out of earshot before she returned her attention to Jake. "Sarah's Trey Sanford's P.R. rep," she explained.

"What did she mean about you joining the enemy?"

"We met last year when I was watching from the Sanford hauler. Trey Sanford had gotten me a pass."

"How do you know Trey?"

"We went out a few times."

"You told me you're not dating anyone."

"I'm not. Trey and I stopped seeing each other months ago." She tilted her head to one side as she studied him. The stray lock of hair slid over her eye again. "Does that bother you?"

"What? Why should it?"

"Oh, I don't know. Maybe you're jealous?"

Did the urge to clamp his arm around her, hold her to his side and growl at any man who came near her count as jealousy? "I've got no right to be jealous."

"Why's your cheek twitching?"

He breathed deeply a few times and made an effort to relax his jaw. "It's not."

"Maybe you believe you should protect me from any man I might feel interested in."

With the tip of his index finger he brushed her hair away from her eye. "That would be unreasonable. I'd think that most women your age would be interested in a handsome and fit young man who does something exciting like race cars for a living."

"That's what I thought, too, at first."

"Then what happened? Why did you dump him?"

"No one got dumped. It was mutual. Neither of us felt anything special."

Yes! he thought, grinning inside. "That's a shame," he deadpanned.

"Oh, really? Then it wouldn't bother you if I decided to leave you here and went trolling around the track for someone else?"

He knew she was baiting him, and it was working. He couldn't even think of some other man standing this close to her, inhaling her scent and feeling the warmth of her skin beneath his fingertips. Man, he had it bad. He eased her stray hair back under her hat brim, then cupped her face with his palm. "Is that what you want to do, Becky?"

"There are a lot of things I want, Jake. Finding my birth family is my priority. Finding a man wasn't high on my list. And even if I did want one, you've done an excellent job of pointing out why he shouldn't be you."

"Did it work?"

She sighed and pressed her cheek against his hand. "No."

If he was smart, he would stop this now. Any relationship between them couldn't go anywhere. He'd warned her. He'd done his best to warn himself, too.

But, hell, he was only human. He'd held off while he was investigating her, but now that he wasn't, he didn't think he could fight this attraction anymore. So what if they only spent a few months together, or a few weeks? As long as neither of them had any illusions, what harm could it do? He stroked his thumb along her cheekbone. "Good."

"Good?"

"Yeah. I did miss you, Becky. I thought about you the

whole time you were gone even though I shouldn't have. The truth is, if Kent hadn't given you that pass, I would have found some other way to spend the day with you."

She smiled. "So is this a date?"

"I guess it is."

"I'm glad."

"You shouldn't be. This only goes to prove I'm not a nice guy."

"I'll take my chances."

There was a sudden roar of engines from the direction of the track. The debris had been cleared, allowing the cars to resume the race. "Hey, look," Jake said, raising his voice over the increased noise. "There's the green flag. The caution's over."

She didn't glance at the track. "It's about time."

THE GRANDSTAND had emptied hours ago and the haulers had left the racetrack in a gleaming, two-by-two convoy, yet the infield wasn't yet empty. The air was ripe with the smell of beer, grilling meat and the muggy heat of a July night. Warmth continued to radiate from the ground, as well as from the barbecue that had been set up outside Dean and Patsy Grosso's luxuriously spacious motor home. The toe-tapping beat of country music underscored the sounds of lively conversation from the fair-size crowd around the food table. Instead of packing up and clearing out as soon as the race ended, the Grosso family, along with most of the Cargill-Grosso team that had worked the race, were letting off steam.

Ice cubes rattled as Jake dug through the bottom of one of the coolers beside the picnic tables. He came up with a club soda, wiped the can on his pant leg and handed it to Becky. "Are you sure you wouldn't rather have a beer?" he asked, fishing out a can of beer for himself.

She popped the soda open and took a long drink. "Not

if I plan to have some of that sausage. It smells too good to pass up."

"Glad to see you don't stick to rabbit food all the time."

"I tried, but lettuce doesn't barbecue well. I found that it tends to fall through the grill."

Jake laughed, and Becky felt a surge of warmth that had nothing to do with the temperature. She had smiled so much today her cheeks were getting sore, yet she couldn't seem to stop. Watching the race with Jake had been wonderful. He was extremely knowledgeable about all the teams, not only Cargill-Grosso, and she had seen that he'd been into the action as much as she had. She couldn't remember enjoying a race more.

Still, it hadn't only been the fact that Kent had finished in second place that had made her this happy. It was because she and Jake were together.

Something had shifted between them as they'd shared the excitement of today's race. Not that their priorities had changed—they'd both been up-front with each other about what they wanted. She suspected they'd been overreacting when they'd worried about where this attraction might lead, or whether it would lead anywhere. After all, she'd just had a great time watching the race. Now she was having a good time with a man she liked, so what harm could that do? Jake had been true to his word when he'd said he wanted to spend the day with her. And so when he'd headed for the Grossos' motor home at the track for their postrace barbecue, he'd invited her along.

Well, not immediately. He wouldn't have been Jake if he hadn't been concerned about her feelings over the prospect of meeting the rest of the Grossos. She'd pointed out that she'd already met Kent, and that they'd already mingled with most of the Cargill-Grosso team, so going to the family barbecue as Jake's date wouldn't be that big a deal. She'd reasoned that if it turned out she wasn't Gina, then at least she would have had the chance to meet the rest of the members of a legendary racing dynasty. Any fan would jump at an opportunity like that.

And if she did turn out to be Gina, then Jake's caution would be moot anyway. These people would be her family. She would be spending as much time with them as she wanted.

What was there *not* to smile about?

"You look familiar. Have we met before?"

Becky turned and found herself face-to-face with a dark-haired, middle-aged man. He was slightly shorter than her, although his broad shoulders and self-confident posture gave him a presence that made him appear taller. She knew who he was—she'd seen Dean Grosso's face countless times on television and at a distance on the track—yet they had never met.

At least, not that she remembered. They might have met thirty-one years ago, though. In the delivery room at a Nashville hospital.

This man could be her father.

Becky felt Jake's arm settle around her shoulders. His touch steadied her enough for her to smile and extend her hand. "Hello, Mr. Grosso. I'm Becky Peters."

He took her hand in a firm clasp while he studied her face. "Hi, Becky. Call me Dean."

"Becky's a friend of mine from Charlotte," Jake said. "We were watching the race together."

"I hope you don't mind that I came along to your barbecue," Becky added.

"No, of course not. You're more than welcome." He glanced at Jake. "My wife's always trying to get him to bring a date. It's about time."

"Funny, I said that to him, too," Becky said.

Dean returned his attention to Becky. His forehead furrowed. "So, have we met before, Becky?"

"Not that I remember."

"Then you must look like someone I know. I've heard people say that everyone has a double somewhere."

"You might have seen Becky's picture," Jake said. "She's a model."

Dean raised his eyebrows. "Oh?"

"There are ads all over the place with Becky modeling blue jeans."

"I guess that explains it. You're certainly lovely enough to be a model, Becky."

"Thank you. All the credit for that goes to my parents."

A trim, blue-eyed woman moved to Dean's side and slipped her hand through the crook of his elbow. "Did I just hear you calling someone lovely?"

Even if Becky hadn't recognized the woman's face from NASCAR coverage, she would have known this was Patsy Grosso by the way she fit so perfectly next to Dean. The couple had gone through a rocky period in their marriage but had reconciled last year. It was obvious by their body language they adored each other.

Becky's adoptive parents had broken up more times than she could have counted. Their reconciliations hadn't lasted long. The brief periods of peace in the house had been laced with tension that would continue to build until the next argument.

Oh, how she'd wished her parents could have been like the Grossos.

It was mind-boggling to think that this couple actually *could* be her parents.

Dean's face softened into a smile as he leaned over to give his wife a kiss. "You did, Patsy. This is Becky Peters, Jake's date."

Patsy smiled and shook Becky's hand. "My husband was

right. You're a beautiful young woman. Jake, why haven't you brought her around before?"

"Becky does a lot of traveling for her work," he replied.

"Becky's a model," Dean said. "Jeans."

Patsy's gaze sharpened. "You're the woman in the jeans posters!" she exclaimed. "Imagine that, we have a celebrity in our midst."

Becky was startled that Patsy would consider *her* a celebrity when Dean and Kent were so famous. The Grossos must be down-to-earth people, she thought happily. They would probably welcome their daughter no matter who she was. "The campaign is getting a lot of good placements."

"Those ads are everywhere. No wonder I thought I'd seen you before."

"It's a common reaction," Jake said. "Happens a lot."

He was right, Becky thought. She often met people who knew her face because of her ads. Yet she couldn't help thinking there might be more to the recognition Dean and Patsy had felt.

Did they see a resemblance to themselves or someone in their family? Or perhaps they sensed a blood tie. Could they really be her parents?

She'd been excited by the possibility for months, but there was a huge difference between merely thinking about it and meeting the couple in person, feeling their palms against hers as they shook her hand, watching them smile, hearing their voices…

Oh, God, yes. She wanted to be their daughter. *Please, let it be true.*

To have a mother again, someone to hold when the world got mean, or even when things were good. Someone who would listen to her fears without laughing and wouldn't be afraid to say what she thought. Or say nothing, if that's what she wanted. It wouldn't matter what her mother did, as long as she was there. And, oh, to have a father who was here where she could see him and be part of his life instead of on the other side of the world with his new wife and family. And what would it be like to have a sister to share secrets with, and a brother to lean on, and a place where she was always welcome?

Becky yearned for that so much that it hurt. It had been too long since she had felt that she belonged. That she wasn't alone. That she was *loved*.

Jake moved his arm from her shoulders to her waist and eased her more firmly against his side. She leaned into him, grateful for his presence and for his support. He'd warned her all along this might be hard on her emotions. She hadn't realized until now how right he'd been.

The conversation turned to the day's race and Kent's chances for the rest of the season. Somehow Becky managed to contribute comments at the appropriate time, but it was almost a relief when the Grossos moved away. Jake leaned over to look at her face, then without another word left his beer on the nearest table and gently steered her past the barbecue and around to the rear of the motor home.

The huge vehicle blocked much of the noise and most of the light that was centered over the barbecue. There were other motor homes still in the lot, but the people around them were either having small parties of their own or making preparations to leave. No one appeared to pay any attention to Becky and Jake, leaving them in relative privacy. "Are you okay?" he asked.

Becky pulled away from him and leaned her backside against the bumper. "To be honest, I'm a bit overwhelmed."

"Meeting the Grossos wasn't as easy as you thought, was it?"

"No, it wasn't. Meeting Kent last week was one thing, but being face-to-face with the couple who might have borne me…" She rolled her soda can along her forehead, focusing on the cool metal against her skin. "I know in my head that nothing might come of this, but my heart's not listening. I want so badly to believe they're my family."

"Yeah, I was afraid of that. I shouldn't have brought you here."

She grasped his hand. "No, Jake. I'm glad you did. The Grossos are wonderful people. My feelings might be mixed up, but they're nice feelings."

"You sure?"

"Positive. However this turns out, I can't regret trying."

"I remember you mentioned that before. You told me you can't see keeping your heart safe if it means it never gets used."

She blinked. Had she said that? Probably. It's what she believed. "You have a phenomenal memory."

"At times. But overall I find my brain hasn't been functioning all that reliably around you."

Although his face was in shadow, she could see the beginning of a smile. She tugged him forward until he turned around to lean against the bumper beside her. "As far as I'm concerned, you've been terrific," she said. "Thanks."

"Geez, you're not going to start telling me I'm a nice guy again, are you? That's embarrassing."

She realized he was trying to lighten her mood. As far as she was concerned, that only proved that he *was* nice. "What do you want to be, Jake?"

"Where should I begin? How about seventeen years younger?"

"You've got a real hang-up about this age difference between us, but it didn't seem to bother your cousin or her husband. They both seemed happy that you brought a date."

"They might not have been that open-minded if they thought you were their daughter."

"Nonsense." She leaned forward to set her soda on the ground by her feet, then reached up to smooth back Jake's hair. "You're an attractive man. And as much as you try to deny it, you're sensitive and considerate, too. Any woman would be lucky to go out with you, but from the sound of things, you haven't been dating anyone lately. Why is that?"

"Hey, we were talking about you. How did this get to be about me?"

She dropped her hand. "Why are you avoiding the question, Jake?"

"There's nothing much to say. I'm not a monk, Becky, but most women want a relationship to go somewhere and I'm not a settling-down kind of guy. Especially not at my age. I thought you realized that."

The answer was too glib, Becky thought. Anyway, she didn't believe it. Yes, Jake had told her weeks ago that he was a confirmed bachelor, yet he had struck her as a responsible man, one who sincerely cared about people. She was sure he would take any relationship seriously. "You seem to get along well with the Grossos. What about the rest of your family? Your mother and your brothers?"

"I don't see them much. Two of my brothers went to live in California and the other one moved to Portland. Our mother remarried years ago, before I joined the army. She and her husband are in Denver now. He takes good care of her."

A silence fell between them. Becky became aware of voices around the other side of the motor home and the occasional clink of cutlery, but she and Jake were still alone. She slid closer to him. "You keep in touch with them, don't you?"

"Oh, sure. E-mail, telephone. We're busy but we haven't lost track. My sisters-in-law send me stacks of pictures of all my nieces and nephews. Not as many as your mother took of you, but they're still working on it."

"Haven't you ever wanted children of your own?"

He stretched out his bad leg and rubbed his knee. "I told you, I'm not the settling-down type."

"I know that's what you said, but it's not an answer."

"Whoa, all I did was bring you to a barbecue. Maybe in some culture I don't know about that's akin to a marriage proposal, but the last I heard—"

She swatted his arm before he could derail the topic into a joke. "I've been totally honest with you, Jake. Can't you trust me enough to do the same?"

Even in the shadows, she could see the flash of discomfort on his face. She knew it couldn't have been from her swat. It had to have been from what she'd said. "That's it, isn't it?" she murmured. "You don't want to trust me."

"You're making way too much of this, Becky."

"I think you're cautious about everything, including people. You don't want to take chances."

"There's nothing wrong with being careful."

"Maybe not in your job. Being methodical and wanting to make sure of your facts makes you a good detective. It probably made you a good soldier."

He gestured toward his leg. "Not good enough."

"You told me that was an accident."

"There were warning signs I should have picked up on. There was debris on the road. We hadn't taken the time to secure the load properly. Between the smoke and the dust, the visibility was next to nil. Looking back on it, the accident could have been avoided if I'd been more cautious. I've learned the hard way that caution's a good thing, Becky."

She placed her hand on his knee. She could feel the ridges of scar tissue through his pant leg and she thought yet again how much he must have endured. Was this why he didn't like to take chances, either in his business or his personal life? What did she know about how deeply a trauma could affect someone? It was a testament to Jake's character that he'd remained such a sensitive and considerate man in spite of it. No wonder she was falling in love with him...

She withdrew her hand, shaken by what she'd just thought. She must be wrong. She couldn't go from a crush to love in a matter of days. Her emotions had to be scrambled from getting that DNA sample taken and meeting the Grossos. Yes, that was it. Only minutes ago she'd been thinking about how much she longed to be loved. She was probably projecting those feelings onto Jake.

She was attracted to him. They were having a good time together. She shouldn't confuse that with something deeper.

"I'm sorry," she said, shoving herself off the bumper. "You were right, all you did was invite me to a barbecue. That doesn't give me the right to interrogate you like this."

He caught her wrist. "Do you still want an answer?"

"Answer?"

He rose to his feet. "You wanted to know why I'm single."

"It's okay, Jake. You don't have to—"

"It's not a secret. All the Grossos know about this, so you might as well, too. Not that I'm saying you're a Grosso."

Of course, he had to add that qualifier, she thought. That's just the way he was.

"I did plan to get married once," he said. He released her wrist and raked his hand through his hair. "As corny as it sounds, she had been my childhood sweetheart. Heather and I were engaged for years, but it didn't work out. It made me realize I wasn't cut out for marriage."

She took a minute to absorb what he'd said. He'd been engaged. That made sense. A broken engagement, especially with a woman he'd loved since childhood, would have had a profound effect on a man as cautious as Jake. It could have influenced his outlook as much as his injury had.

But his revelation only led to more questions. Had he loved Heather? He must have or he wouldn't have wanted to marry her, but did he still love her? That could be a reason he hadn't married someone else. What had happened to break them up? How could any woman have thrown away a chance for a future with a man like Jake?

Or it could be the other way around. Jake could have been the one who had ended the engagement, yet Becky didn't think so. There was something in his tone that hinted at buried pain. It was similar to the way he sounded when he spoke of his injury.

"I'm sorry," she said. "That must have been difficult."

He shrugged. "It was a long time ago. I don't normally think about it, but you wanted me to be honest with you."

"I appreciate that, Jake."

"But I didn't take you away from the party so I could talk about my past."

She glanced around. "Yes, I realize that," she said, stepping away. "You were only trying to calm me down after my meeting with the Grossos. I'm sorry."

"Will you stop apologizing?" He hooked his arm around her waist before she could retreat any farther. "Anyway, I didn't find us some privacy just so you could de-stress, either."

"You didn't?"

"Nope." He eased her closer. "I had another reason for getting you alone."

"What?"

"This," he said, lowering his mouth to hers.

At the first contact of his lips, her thoughts were submerged beneath a wave of sensation. The kiss was gentle, at odds with his grasp on her waist. She could feel his restraint in the way his arms hardened and his breath puffed hot across her cheek. Tension hummed through his body to hers, sparking from every point where they touched, yet his lips remained soft and giving.

Becky had been kissed more skillfully. She'd been kissed in settings that were far more romantic than the back of a motor home at a racetrack. She'd had kisses that were meant as a passionate prelude to sex.

Yet she'd never experienced the sense of connection to another person that she did now.

It had always been that way with Jake. The tingles she'd felt when they'd first met, and the breath-stealing thrill when he'd held her last week, were nothing compared to the pleasure of his mouth moving against hers.

He tilted his head until he found the best angle, then fitted more confidently against her, savoring the contact. He didn't kiss as if he were still in love with his old fiancée. He kissed her as if they were the only two people in the world. Time stretched around them as he invited her to join him in this first exploration. She did. After weeks of restraining her desire to do this, she was almost giddy with the freedom of finally being able to indulge.

His lips moved into a smile as he felt her response, yet he didn't take the kiss further. He seemed to understand that for here, for now, this was all the intimacy either of them needed.

It might not be love, but it felt right. Perfect. It felt like coming home.

Becky pulled back her head, breaking the kiss, and stared at Jake.

He smiled, touching his finger to the moisture on her lower lip. "You didn't hit me again. I guess that's a good sign."

It took a moment to catch her breath. "It was nice, Jake."

His smile turned to a grimace. "Nice? Ouch."

She realized the word hadn't come close to describing that incredible kiss, but it might be better not to expand on it. How could she hope to express what she was feeling when she didn't understand it herself?

CHAPTER SEVEN

RALPH BOCCI didn't bother to muffle his footsteps as he strode down the hall to McMasters's office. He knew the routine in this building well enough to know there was no one else here at this time of night. And ever since he managed to lift a skeleton key from one of the cleaning crew, getting into the office was a snap.

Not that he was going to tell the Brown witch. No, if she thought this job was getting easier, she'd probably step up her threats about talking to his parole officer. The woman must take pleasure in controlling men. How did her husband put up with her? Back in the day, Hank Brown had been hell on wheels. That's what the word around the Shillington plant was. He'd driven for old man Shillington's NASCAR team but had quit cold when he'd married Cynthia. Traded in his car for a desk and a piece of the family fortune. Come to think of it, the Shillington money would go a long way to sweetening any deal.

Ralph popped a fresh stick of gum into his mouth, closed the door behind him and walked to McMasters's desk to turn on the lamp. The box of baby pictures was still in the corner—he'd looked through them on Mrs. Brown's orders, but it had been a waste of time. So had following the guy around to racetracks. If that was all it took to be a private investigator, maybe Ralph would look into trying his own hand at it once he was through with this job. He glanced at the storage cabinet. Yeah, maybe he'd come back on his own time and help himself to some of the equipment he'd found on the shelves in there. It must be worth a few grand. He could consider it a bonus for everything he'd had to put up with.

As usual, there was nothing on the desk that Mrs. Brown would be interested in, only some rent receipts and a few take-out slips from a diner. Ralph went straight to the filing cabinet, picked the lock and took out the Peters file. A slip of yellow paper that hadn't been there before caught his eye so he tipped it toward the light to get a closer look. At first glance, it appeared to be just another receipt until he noticed there was a name of a laboratory on the top. He squinted to read it more carefully.

Oh, hell, he thought, pulling out his phone. The boss lady wasn't going to be pleased about this.

She wasn't. "A DNA test," she hissed.

"Yeah. I'm pretty sure that's what it means."

"Read it to me again. Don't skip anything."

He did as she ordered, then waited. For once, she seemed to be at a loss for words. When she did speak again, he wished she hadn't. "No way," he said. "I can't do that. I never torched a place."

"You'll do as I say, Mr. Bocci. Need I remind you—"

He broke the connection before she could complete the threat. It was then that he heard the faint sound of voices coming from the other side of the door. Someone was moving down the hall.

Ralph was still holding the yellow paper from the lab. He stuffed it into his pocket along with his phone, replaced the file in the cabinet and dove for the desk to turn off the light. He told himself to stay calm—it could be some of the cleaning crew who had forgotten something. There was a maintenance room at the far end of the hall. That's probably where they were heading. All he had to do was keep quiet until they left.

Whoever was out there was close enough now that Ralph could make out a few words. It was a man and a woman, and they were talking about this weekend's NASCAR Sprint Cup Series race. He caught the name Grosso a few times and his palms began to sweat. He wiped them on his pants and tried to tell himself that it was just a coincidence. Simply because McMasters was investigating the Grosso kidnapping didn't mean anything. Anyone talking about NASCAR was bound to mention the Grossos.

But then Ralph heard the thud of a cane along with the footsteps. He didn't need to look to know who was out there. Of all the rotten luck. What was McMasters doing here now? He glanced at the window behind him, but the opening was filled with the air conditioner. Even if it hadn't been, he didn't much like the idea of going out a second-floor window without a fire escape. He didn't like the idea of being trapped in here, either—he'd had more than his fill of small spaces in prison.

Ralph bit down hard, only to discover he must have swallowed his gum. McMasters was a big guy, in spite of that gimpy leg, and looked like he knew how to handle himself. Ralph wouldn't want to tangle with him. His sole hope was striking first. Nicotine-lined lungs or not, he should be able to outrun a cripple. He dried his palms on his pants again, then pulled his knife from his boot, flicked it open and crept toward the door.

"So, ARE WE ON for the next NASCAR Sprint Cup race in Indianapolis in two weeks?" Jake asked, fishing in his pocket for his keys. The overhead light in the hall had been dimmed for the night. He had to hold up the key ring to pick out the right one.

They'd arrived back in Charlotte several hours later than they'd planned. Thunderstorms in Chicago had delayed their departure, and once they'd made it home, the traffic on the airport parkway had been, well, parked. Yet Becky had enjoyed every minute of her time with Jake. "I'd love to go," she said. "I don't know whether you'd be content to watch from the stands with me. Maybe you could use your connections to get me another pass."

"Maybe."

"I bet Kent would give me one if you asked. I wouldn't get in the way."

"That's true. You might be tall, but you're pretty skinny so you wouldn't take up much space in the pits."

"I am not skinny."

He stuck the key in the lock, propped his cane against the door frame and turned to span her waist with his hands. He demonstrated his point by tapping his thumbs together. "Slender, then."

"That doesn't prove anything. You have big hands."

He tightened his grip and lifted her until her feet left the floor. "You weigh next to nothing."

Laughing, she braced her hands on his shoulders. "And you're showing off."

"Uh-huh. All those bench presses at the gym have to be good for something."

Becky curled her fingers, the better to appreciate the flexing going on beneath his shirt. "I figured that you must work out."

"Yeah, I'm a big believer in exercise." He lowered her slowly until her face was level with his. The tips of her toes still weren't touching the floor. "Some forms are more enjoyable than others."

"Oh? Like what?"

He smiled and wiggled his eyebrows.

Becky knew he was teasing. Apart from their conversation at the Grossos' barbecue, for the remainder of the weekend they'd both kept things light between them.

They'd been flirting, nothing more. So she couldn't believe the wave of heat that raced through her at the thought of more intimate activities with Jake. Except for his hands on her waist and hers on his shoulders, they were barely touching. She wanted more. Much more. "Um, Jake?"

"Yeah?"

"You don't need to prove how strong you are. I already know that."

"Really?"

"All I have to do is watch you move. Aren't you going to put me down?"

His smile turned lopsided. "Seems like we had this conversation before."

"Not exactly, but similar."

"Mmm. I can get used to holding you, Becky. You're not in a hurry, are you?"

She rubbed her heel behind his good leg. This had been such a perfect weekend, she was reluctant to have it end. "I have some plants that need watering, but they'll keep. What about you?"

"Right now, I can't think of anywhere else I'd rather be. Well, maybe somewhere more comfortable," he said, pulling her flush to the front of his body as he leaned back against the door.

The moment his shoulders touched the frosted glass panel, the door swung inward.

Jake swore and lurched to the side as he recovered his balance. He quickly set Becky on her feet. "I didn't turn the key yet," he muttered. "What the—"

His words cut off as the door was pulled open completely from inside. A split second later, a stocky, dark-haired man moved into the doorway. Though the light in the corridor was poor, it was enough to reveal the gleam of a knife in his hand.

Becky cried out a warning but Jake had already shifted sideways and was lifting his forearm to block the attack. In spite of his lame leg, he'd assumed a combat stance. He yelled at her over his shoulder. "Get back! Run!"

She stumbled back a few feet to give him more space, but she had no intention of running away and leaving Jake here alone.

The man in the doorway jabbed with his weapon again. Instead of retreating, Jake reached past him to grasp the door. He yanked it toward them hard, smashing it into his assailant's side.

The wood shuddered and splintered at the impact. The frosted glass in the upper half shattered, sending shards flying everywhere. Momentarily stunned, the man cursed and slashed wildly at Jake's face. The blade passed within a hairbreadth of his ear.

In desperation, Becky glanced around for something she could use as a weapon and spotted Jake's cane on the floor beside the door frame. She darted forward to pick it up, gripping it like a baseball bat.

The next thing she knew, she was knocked facedown on the floor with a crushing weight on her back. Pain knifed through her hand. She struggled to draw in a breath but the smell of stale cigarette smoke made her gag.

"Becky!"

It was Jake's voice. She tried to respond but her reply came out as a moan.

There was the sound of flesh hitting flesh. Something clattered to the floor and suddenly, the weight on her back disappeared. "Becky! Are you okay?"

She lifted her head. Jake's attacker staggered against the side of the corridor. Blood flowed from his nose. The knife he'd been wielding was on the floor at Jake's feet. She gasped and scrambled to her knees to reach for it.

Jake glanced at her over his shoulder, his face hard. "Stay back. Don't touch it."

The moment's distraction was all the other man needed. He shoved himself away from the wall and sprinted for the staircase. Seconds later, his footsteps thudded down the stairs.

Jake swore under his breath.

Becky wobbled to her feet. "Are you all right?"

He spun to face her. "I'm fine. Don't worry about me." He reached out to run his hands along her arms and over her shoulders. "Are you okay? Does anything hurt?"

Her chest ached with every breath and her palms stung but her first concern was Jake. She shook her head, her gaze racing over him. There was blood on his shirt. "Oh, my God. You're bleeding. We have to get you to a hospital."

He looked down. "It's not my blood," he said. "It's his."

She forced herself to focus. The front of his shirt was covered with dark splatters but the fabric didn't appear to have been cut.

Jake pulled her into his arms. For a while, he simply held her, his breathing as ragged as hers. "It's okay, Becky. It's over. He's gone."

She nodded against his shoulder. "We have to call the police."

"We will."

"Who was he? What did he want?"

Jake smoothed his palm over her hair. "I don't think he wanted to hurt us."

"He had a *knife*. My God, Jake. He could have killed you."

"Not really. He wasn't very good."

She shuddered and lifted her head to look past him. The corridor was still empty. There were no sounds from the stairs, but... "Jake, we can't stay here!" she said, stepping out of his embrace. "What if he comes back?"

"That's unlikely. He had no way of knowing we'd be

here tonight so we couldn't have been his target. He probably just fought because he wanted to get away."

On some level, she knew he was making sense, but she was having a hard time calming down enough to listen. "Are you sure you're all right?"

"Come on," he said, taking her hand. "You'd better sit down."

The moment he touched her hand, she cried out. Jake caught both her wrists and turned her palms upward. Blood oozed from the base of her right thumb where an inch-long sliver of glass protruded from her skin.

"Damn, you must have picked that up when you fell. I'm sorry, Becky."

Her stomach rolled threateningly as she looked at her injury. The light in the hall was too dim for her to have noticed it before. She hadn't felt anything until he'd touched it. She averted her eyes and swallowed hard. "Pull it out."

"No, not yet. It could be the reason you're not bleeding worse. I'm sorry," he repeated.

"Why? It wasn't your fault."

"Yes, it was. I hadn't known you were behind me when I threw that guy. He landed on top of you."

"I thought you might have needed my help…" She didn't try explaining any further. Jake hadn't needed her help. If she'd been thinking straight she would have remembered that he'd been trained by the Special Forces. If she'd stayed out of the way as he'd wanted her to, she wouldn't have been hurt and Jake would probably have been able to restrain the man. She blew out a shaky breath. "It all happened so fast."

"Yeah. Sneak attacks usually do." He retrieved his cane and led her past the wood splinters and broken glass on the floor to guide her to one of the armchairs in his office. As soon as he was assured that she was comfortable, he turned on his desk lamp and grabbed his phone. His call to the police was brief.

Becky started to protest when she heard him request an ambulance but the look he gave her was so intense she fell silent.

Now that the shock was wearing off, her aches felt worse. So did her sense of uneasiness. It was true that the attack had happened quickly. The whole thing couldn't have lasted more than a minute. Yet now every vivid, terrifying detail replayed in her mind, as if in slow motion. She cradled her hand on her lap and anchored herself by keeping her focus on Jake. He retrieved a clean towel from his gym bag and wrapped it gently around her glass sliver to immobilize it. He knew what he was doing. They were both safe. That's what mattered. Still, Becky had the niggling feeling that she was missing something important.

JAKE MOVED into the corridor, too wired to remain still. He'd done his best to minimize the incident for Becky's sake, but he was worried. The man with the knife hadn't been large enough or skilled enough to pose much difficulty for Jake, but he'd been desperate, and desperate people were always the most dangerous. They didn't behave rationally. So it was with some relief that Jake saw Lieutenant Denning had arrived and was speaking with one of the uniformed policemen who had been the first on the scene. Positioning himself near the remains of the office door so that he could keep an eye on Becky, Jake waved Len over.

"Thanks for coming out," Jake said.

Len suppressed a yawn. He looked like an unmade bed, but then, that's probably where he'd been when he'd received Jake's call. "No problem. You sounded in rough shape."

"I'm fine. It could have been a lot worse. Did you see the blade?"

"One of the uniforms collected it. You told him no one else had touched it, is that right?"

"Yeah. You should get a few good prints."

"So, what happened?"

Jake glanced at Becky to check the paramedic's progress and saw that her wound was already being bandaged. They had deemed it too minor to warrant moving her to a hospital, which agreed with what she'd told Jake, but he'd wanted to be sure. Any wound not properly tended could get infected and scar. That could prove a problem in Becky's line of work.

Who was he kidding? It wasn't her livelihood that concerned him, it was her life. Just the thought of her having been exposed to this level of danger was making him crazy.

"Buddy, are you still with me?"

Jake returned his attention to Len and gave him a detailed summary of the attack.

"What's your take on this?" Len asked when Jake had finished. "Burglary gone wrong?"

Jake shook his head. "If I'd thought that's all it was, I wouldn't have phoned you. I would have let the uniforms handle it."

Len twisted to look at the door beside Jake's office. "I don't know, Jake. The drugs that would be in that dentist's office and the electronic equipment in yours would look pretty attractive to a thief."

"I've gone through my office. Nothing's missing."

"You interrupted him."

"Obviously. I think he was after information."

"Any idea what?"

Jake looked at Becky again. The paramedic had finished his work. Becky turned her wrist from one side to the other as if testing the movement. The bandage had been wrapped across her palm and around her hand, but it didn't appear to be causing her any discomfort.

"Am I boring you? Maybe you'd prefer to go give your friend a kiss and make it better."

Jake jerked his gaze back to Len. "That's Becky Peters. Her adoptive father is Floyd Peters."

"Peters? Right, the punk with the assault record you asked me about. Do you think he did this?"

"No. He lives in Australia, and I've seen pictures of him. It definitely wasn't him. But I'd bet money that this is connected with the Gina Grosso case. None of my other open cases would inspire someone to take a risk like this."

"Maybe Peters hired him."

"That's a possibility. But I don't believe Peters would have wanted Becky to get hurt."

"That doesn't rule him out. From what you told me, she was collateral damage."

Jake saw that the paramedic was gathering his supplies and repacking his case. Becky had already stood and was moving toward the door. He held out his free arm as she approached. "How are you feeling?" he asked.

"Fine."

"And your hand?"

"The gash is clean and taped closed. It wasn't that deep. Are you okay?"

He nodded as he studied her face. Now that the surge of adrenaline from the attack had worn off, she was beginning to show signs of exhaustion. He draped his arm around her shoulders and drew her to his side before he introduced her to Len. "Could you let me know if you come up with anything on those prints?" he asked.

"Sure thing." Len suppressed another yawn. "It still could be you're making too much of this. The perp might have been high and mistook your office for the dentist's next door."

Becky stiffened. "The dentist," she said. "That man."

Jake looked at her. "What is it?"

"Now I remember. He smelled like cigarettes. I saw him before."

"Where?"

"Here. The day before I left for Italy. He was waiting outside your office but he left as soon as I spoke to him. I'd thought he was waiting for the dentist and had changed his mind."

Jake firmed his hold on Becky and exchanged a look with Len. His friend nodded, obviously grasping the significance of what Becky had said. The break-in hadn't been random. Whoever had done it had known exactly which office he'd wanted to target.

And he'd probably done it before, Jake thought. The man could have been following his progress for weeks. If Floyd Peters was behind it, Jake had badly underestimated him. How far would Peters and his accomplice go to keep Becky's origins a secret?

As it turned out, Jake got his answer sooner than he'd expected. The radios of both the police officer down the hall and the paramedic in the office crackled to life within seconds of each other. Jake couldn't make out what was said, but whatever it was sent both of them racing for the staircase. Moments later, Len's cell phone trilled.

"What's going on?" Jake demanded.

Len said a few words into his phone and flipped it shut. "Four-alarm fire in the hospital zone."

"My God," Becky said. "All those people…"

"The fire hasn't reached the hospital itself yet," Len said. "It's centered in an analytical laboratory."

CHAPTER EIGHT

JAKE PUT THE PHONE on his desk and rolled his shoulders, trying to ease the kink in the back of his neck. His body was screaming for rest, but apart from the two hours he'd snatched at his apartment after he'd driven Becky home early this morning, it had been more than a day since he'd slept. The way things were shaping up, it might be another day before he did again.

According to what the fire department had just told him, the preliminary investigation of the blaze in the laboratory confirmed it had been deliberately set. All of the analyses that had been in progress had been destroyed, including the DNA samples that Nicole had sent there the previous week. It hadn't been the fire alone that had ruined them. The arsonist had taken the time to trash the place before he'd poured gasoline over everything.

The arson occurring so soon after the break-in here couldn't have been a coincidence. The receipt for the DNA test, which had the lab's address printed on it, was missing from Becky's file. Someone wanted to keep the truth from coming out.

Yet destroying the test samples was only a temporary solution. It would be easy to arrange for a second test.

Jake leaned back in his chair, his gaze going to the sheet of plywood that was serving as a temporary door. Was Peters really behind what had happened here and at the lab?

Destroying the lab had involved a level of violence far beyond break-and-enter and would carry a heavier penalty. Peters had been a hothead when he'd been a kid, but he'd been clean since he'd married Lizzie. None of his early brushes with the law had involved anything premeditated. Still, it might be possible he'd know how to contact the kind of lowlife who wouldn't have hesitated to do both crimes.

It all depended on how desperate Peters was. He had good reason to be concerned about possible abduction charges, since the FBI had reopened the Gina Grosso kidnapping case. Yet Jake had been hired to find Gina, not to bring her abductors to justice. The Grossos weren't interested in vengeance. They simply wanted to be reunited with their lost child. When they'd approached him about taking the case, they had already had their fill of legal proceedings because they'd been dealing with the murder of their friend...

The hair at the back of Jake's neck stood up. He sucked in his breath. The murder of Alan Cargill last December had appeared to be a crime of opportunity rather than premeditation. At first it had seemed like a mugging, but then suspicions had arisen that Alan's death had been tied to an old scandal about cheating in NASCAR. So far, no proof of any link to the cheating scandal had been found.

Were the police looking in the wrong direction? The allegations about Gina being alive had surfaced around the same time that Alan had been killed. Had the timing of that been merely coincidence?

Alan Cargill had been stabbed to death.

The man who had been spying on Jake had wielded a knife. Was that a coincidence, too?

Maybe the fire in the lab hadn't been intended as a solution. It could have been meant as a warning.

Jake rocked forward to yank open the top drawer of his

desk. He grabbed his Rolodex and flipped through the cards until he found Lucas Haines's number.

The New York detective answered on the second ring. "Haines."

"Lucas, it's Jake McMasters."

"Hey, Jake. What can I do for you?"

"I'm calling about the Alan Cargill case. Are you any closer to an arrest yet?"

"Unfortunately, no. Seems I get a lead only to find something to rule it out."

"Yeah, I know what you mean."

"I take it there's a reason you're asking."

"There have been some developments here in Charlotte I believe you should know about."

"I thought you were looking into the Grosso kidnapping."

"I am. The two crimes might be related."

"What makes you think that?"

Jake gave Lucas a rundown of his progress on the Grosso case as well as a summary of the events of the previous night. Only then did he detail his suspicions. He finished by giving Lucas Len's phone number. "Lieutenant Denning is having the knife tested for prints," Jake said. "He told me he'll know later today whether or not he gets a hit on them. I'll ask him to call you."

"Good. Thanks." Lucas was silent for a moment. "Wait a minute." There was the sound of papers being shuffled in the background. "Gina starts with a *G*."

"Right. Why?"

"Cargill made an entry in his electronic organizer the night he died. 'Ask D. about G.'"

Jake's hand tightened around the phone. "The *G* could stand for Gina."

"There was no reason for me to consider it before. Dean Grosso had told me that during their last conversation, Cargill had asked him about GranolaPlus. It's a cereal company that was interested in sponsoring Kent. I'd concluded that *D* referred to Dean and *G* meant GranolaPlus. That explained the BlackBerry entry on your electronic organizer."

"Maybe not."

"Maybe not," Lucas repeated. "Jake, I appreciate your co-operation. If you find anything else that might help, call me."

"Count on it."

"And, Jake?"

"Yeah?"

"Until we sort this out, you might want to exercise some extra caution."

Jake had to flex his fingers a few times after he put down the phone. He'd been holding it so tightly his hand had cramped. Caution? Becky had said he was too cautious, but when it came to her, he'd been worrying about the wrong things. He snatched the receiver once more and dialed Len's number.

"Um, Becky?" Tara Dalton set two glasses on the counter of Becky's tiny kitchen. "Are you sure you should be having any of this in your condition?"

Becky made a face at her friend and jabbed the button on the blender. Her friends had meant well when they'd come over to check on her, but Becky needed company and the distraction of a girls' night more than she needed sympathy. "I'm fine," she said over the noise. "I didn't take any meds except an aspirin and that was early this morning. Nicole, tell her."

Nicole squeezed past her to position a lime on the cutting board. "It's okay, Tara. Becky's right. Alcohol in moderation won't hurt."

"It's for medicinal purposes anyway," Becky said. She shut off the blender. "I tried napping but I've been jumpy all day. I could use some loosening up."

"You're still feeling the aftereffects of that attack," Nicole said.

"I don't know why. Jake's the one who fought the guy off."

"Doesn't matter. It'll take a while for the memory to fade." Nicole sliced the lime in half. "It's perfectly normal so don't worry."

"That's a low-cal lime, right, Nicole?"

She laughed. "Absolutely. And as long as we stand up while we drink, there are no calories in the margaritas."

"Well, I think you're holding up well, considering," Tara said. "How's your wrist?"

"I can barely feel it." Becky held up her bandaged hand and extended the fingers of her other hand toward it as if she were modeling a pair of gloves. "I don't have another job until Thursday. Lucky for me, it's modeling jeans so the bruises on my knees won't show. I should be able to get rid of this gauze by then."

"As long as the wound's healing all right and you're sensible," Nicole said.

"I wouldn't have been hurt at all if I'd stayed out of Jake's way. He was amazing."

"Amazing?"

"Awesome. He's very strong, you know."

"No, I didn't realize that. He looks so harmless."

"Mmm, I wouldn't describe him like that. Under those loose shirts he wears he's all muscle. He's got great body control, too."

Tara reached up to take a third glass from the cupboard and set it beside the blender. "So is he Harrison Ford or George Clooney?"

Nicole raised her eyebrows. "What's this?"

"Becky said that's who Jake reminded her of."

"She did? That's interesting, but I can't say I noticed any resemblance."

"It was more that he reminded her of the characters they played," Tara explained.

"You should have seen how worried she looked when she thought something might have happened to him," Nicole said.

"When was that?" Tara demanded.

"Last week, when I met her at the airport."

"Hmm, that *is* interesting. I wonder what it means."

Becky propped her hands on her hips. "Ladies, I'm right here. Stop talking about me as if I'm not."

"Then talk to us," Tara said. "Tell us what's going on with you and Jake."

"I suppose we're seeing each other."

"You suppose? What does that mean?"

"We had a great time together in Chicago over the weekend. He's a really nice guy."

"But?" Nicole prodded.

Becky felt her cheeks heat. She picked up a slice of lime and rubbed it around the rim of a glass, then dipped the glass in the bowl of salt. "It's kind of complicated."

"Why?"

"It's the Gina thing. My feelings are probably confused."

"What do you mean?"

Becky handed the glass to Tara and prepared another. "I like him a lot. I feel good when I'm around him because he's smart, funny and incredibly sensitive. He's self-confident, too, without being pushy about it."

"He struck me as a responsible man," Nicole said.

"Oh, he's that, all right. From the moment I met him, I felt I could trust him. We had this…connection. I don't know what else to call it."

"I'm still not seeing a downside," Tara said.

These were her best friends, Becky thought. They'd shared all the ups and downs of their lives with each other, and she trusted them like the sisters she'd never had. Why was she hesitating to share her feelings for Jake?

Maybe because she still hadn't figured them out. She fixed a glass for herself and poured the margaritas. "I've got a serious crush on him," she admitted finally. "But it might be mixed up with the whole business of finding my family."

Nicole sipped her drink. "You've got a point. Trying to find out who you are has to be stirring up some powerful emotions."

"It is. This just isn't the right time for me to be thinking about a man."

"Is there ever a right time?" Tara asked. "Romance was the last thing on my mind when I met Adam."

"When it's right, it's right," Nicole said. "You and Adam Sanford were meant to be."

Tara smiled. "That's true, but my love life isn't news anymore. We're talking about Becky's. Let's cut to the chase. Is Jake a good kisser?"

Becky had been about to take a drink. She sputtered against the rim of her glass.

"Well?" Tara persisted.

"Yes. He's wonderful. But it's still confusing."

Nicole put her hand on Becky's arm. "For what it's worth, I think you're wise to take things slow. You do have a lot to deal with right now. Because of that fire we'll need to do another DNA test, which is going to drag out the waiting for you again. Once we get the results, you'll need to give yourself time to come to terms with whatever they prove."

"They're going to prove that I *am* Gina. Why else would someone want to sabotage them?"

"That's a good question," Nicole said. "Did you hear anything from the police?"

"The lieutenant handling the case gave me a follow-up

call this morning, but he didn't tell me much. I expect that Jake's busy checking out the other Gina claimants. There were forty-two of them, you know."

"You're kidding! That many?"

"Those are only the ones who have come forward," Becky said. "Who knows how many are out there still hoping for their chance? Any of them could have a partner who was willing to sabotage Jake's investigation."

Tara grasped Becky's shoulder. "You'd better be careful."

"I will be. Anyway, this will all be over once that second test is done."

"That's true," Tara said, squeezing lightly. "But whatever those test results show isn't going to change who you are. I know Nicole told you to take things slow, but if your gut is telling you that Jake's the one, he'll still be the one no matter what your last name turns out to be."

Becky looked from one friend to the other. One of the reasons she loved these women was because they were never afraid to tell each other the truth. In this case, they were both right. Unfortunately, that didn't help sort out her feelings— they were more muddled than ever. She sighed, then lifted her glass and took a long swallow.

"What is it?" Nicole asked. "You look thoughtful."

"I'm trying to decide which we need more, a group hug or another margarita."

They laughed and somehow managed both.

BECKY HADN'T REALIZED she'd fallen asleep until the knock on the door woke her. She pushed her hair off her face and squinted at the clock on her DVD player. It was only a few minutes past ten. Tara and Nicole had cut the evening short and had left her apartment less than twenty minutes ago, saying she needed her sleep. Evidently, they'd been right. She'd nodded off on the couch.

The knocking started again. Becky yawned, rolled to her feet and padded to the door.

Jake's voice came through before she reached it. "Becky! Are you all right?"

She blinked. The urgency in his tone brought her fully awake. "Yes, I'm fine."

"We need to talk. Can I come in?"

"Sure," she said. She straightened her blouse, glanced down to make sure her jeans were fastened and opened the door.

As soon as he crossed the threshold of her apartment, he grasped her arm and gave her a head-to-toe inspection. When he was done, he scowled and turned to lock and chain the door behind him. "Sorry to barge in on you like this but you weren't answering your phone and I got worried."

"I didn't hear it," she said, leading the way to the living room. "When did you call?"

"I've been trying to get you for hours."

"That's funny. I didn't hear…" Her words trailed off as she looked at the answering machine on the hall table. The red light was off. She checked the phone, then smiled weakly. "Sorry. I turned the ringer off in the afternoon. I was trying to get some sleep before my friends came over. It wasn't any use, though. I was too jumpy."

"You had company? They should have let you rest."

"I just told you, I was too restless to sleep. Besides, they're my friends. They knew exactly what I needed, which doesn't include being babied."

He rubbed his face. "Don't be annoyed with me, Becky. I was concerned."

"I'm not annoyed, Jake, but honestly, you didn't need to be concerned. I might not have had combat training like you have, but I'm not made of spun glass."

At the mention of glass, he took her hand so he could look at her bandage. "How's the cut feeling? Any soreness?"

It was a good thing he didn't know about her bruises, she thought. She realized she should be grateful that he was sensitive enough to worry. She'd just been singing his praises to Tara and Nicole. He was a good man. Why did she feel like grinding her teeth? "It's fine. I barely feel it."

He looked at her face, as if checking to see whether or not she was telling the truth.

She sighed. "Jake, you're not still feeling responsible because I was hurt, are you? It wasn't your fault. It was mine for getting in the way."

His forehead furrowed. "Sorry, Becky. I can't help it."

"It's okay. I suspect this protectiveness thing you've got going is hardwired into you."

"You sound disappointed."

"Well, I was hoping there was some other reason you might have come over to see me."

Without another word, he caught her chin in his hand, tipped up her face and kissed her.

Becky's heart skipped, then settled into a heavy throb. Pleasure, pure and simple, washed over her so quickly her knees went weak. She closed her eyes and splayed her fingers on Jake's chest.

It was remarkable how Jake's kisses always felt different. Sometimes they were gentle or playful, other times they were delicious enough to curl her toes. This one was hard to describe. She could feel the fine edge of exhaustion humming through his body, yet there was power in his embrace. The familiar sense of belonging, of home, wrapped around her senses.

This was what she'd needed more than a nap or margaritas. No matter what was happening around them, she always felt better with Jake. She smiled against his mouth, then rested her forehead in the crook of his neck. His scent, the familiar mix of cloves and male skin, surrounded her like an extension of their kiss. "That's better."

He stroked her hair. "I guess I should have done that right away."

"It would have been nice."

"There's that word again."

She laughed softly. "It's because I have trouble finding the right words for you. You're a very complex man, Jake."

"Me? No way. What you see is what you get."

She lifted her head and leaned back so that she could focus on his face. His jaw was darkened with end-of-the-day beard stubble. Although his gaze sparkled with warmth, the skin around his eyes looked taut with weariness. Every one of his forty-eight years showed tonight. That wasn't a bad thing. His age made him look solid and reliable, a man who knew what he wanted and would take all the time he needed to get it. Becky felt a quiver of awareness at the thought.

Oh, yes, she did like what she saw. She smiled and touched his dimple. "Can I get you something? Tea? Some juice? I don't have any beer, but there should be some margarita fixings left."

"No, thanks. I won't stay that long."

The pleasure from their kiss began to ebb. His voice had shifted to his professional tone, the one he'd often used when he'd still been working on her case. "Then you really did come over here just to check up on me."

Instead of replying directly, he took her hand and led her toward the couch. "There's a reason for that, Becky. That's why I need to talk to you."

She sat beside him and curled her feet onto the cushion. "Have they found the man who attacked you?"

"Not yet, but Len got a hit on his fingerprints. It's a man by the name of Ralph Bocci. He's an ex-con. Have you ever heard of him?"

"No. Why should I?"

"You never heard his name mentioned, maybe when you were still living with your father?"

"No, I'm certain I didn't. I had never seen him before that afternoon outside your office. Why?" She pressed backward into the corner of the couch. "You don't think my father put him up to what happened yesterday, do you?"

"I'm sorry, Becky, but I have to consider all the possibilities."

"Well, that's not one of them. My dad never would have asked someone to spy on you. That's not like him. Just because he doesn't approve of me looking for my birth parents doesn't mean he'd do something criminal. Where would he have met someone like this Bocci person, anyway? My dad lives in Melbourne."

"He might have known him in his youth."

"What do you mean, 'in his youth'? My father was never involved with people like that."

Jake glanced away. "The police are still looking for Bocci. He was due to report to his parole officer today but he didn't show up. He's been living in Indianapolis since his release from the state prison ten months ago. His P.O. hadn't known he'd left town."

"Back up a minute. You didn't answer my question. Why did you think my father knew Bocci?"

"I was mixed up."

"No, you weren't. You've got a steel-trap memory. Jake, tell me the truth about my father."

"I'm sorry. I should have guessed you wouldn't have known. Floyd has an arrest record. The most serious was an assault charge arising from a bar fight. He was twenty-one at the time. He moved in some rough circles when he was young."

Her first impulse was to deny it, but she couldn't. What Jake had said had the ring of truth. Her father did have a short fuse, but a lot of people made mistakes in their youth that they regretted later. And as crimes went, a bar fight wasn't that serious. What did it matter that her parents hadn't told her? She shouldn't be surprised. They had both been good at keeping secrets from her. If she was Gina Grosso, then they had lied to her for her entire life. If she was Gina...

She drew up her knees and wrapped her arms around her legs, struck by an ugliness she hadn't wanted to think about before.

"Becky, talk to me. The last thing I wanted to do was hurt your feelings."

She'd been so focused on hoping that she might be Gina, and fantasizing about belonging to the Grosso family, that she had purposely avoided examining the issue of how she'd ended up with the Peters. "You must think I'm an idiot."

"Becky, no." He slid closer and reached out to touch her face but she tipped her head away. He dropped his arm to the back of the couch. "I think you're a very courageous woman."

"It must seem ridiculous for me to get indignant at the idea my father would know a criminal, because if I'm Gina Grosso, then he must be a kidnapper. My mother, too. It doesn't seem possible that the people I knew were capable of that, but they must have been. They stole a baby from her family. That's got to be one of the cruelest things anyone can do. They were criminals."

"If they did steal you, they were desperate."

"I never wanted to consider this. It felt disloyal so I just glossed over it in my mind. Of course my parents wouldn't have wanted me to dig into my origins. What they must have done was despicable."

"They wanted a child. Floyd's arrest record might have kept them from adopting through legal channels."

"So they might have solved that by stealing a newborn baby from the Nashville hospital nursery. My God, Jake. How did Patsy survive a blow like that? How did Dean? How could I even think of being happy about being Gina when it means there was all this suffering connected with my birth?"

"It was over thirty years ago, Becky. Dean and Patsy are strong people. They got past it. All they care about now is finding their child alive."

She pressed her forehead against her knees. "They thought their baby was dead."

"That's what the police told them. It's why Dean stopped looking."

"It's awful."

"Yes, it was a bad time for them. That's why I'm trying to be so careful about getting their hopes up now."

"I'm sorry for giving you a hard time about that."

"It's understandable. I might be hardwired to be protective, but you seem to be hardwired to take chances." He rested his fingers on her forearm. "You're a caring and generous woman, Becky. I admire that. I don't want to see you get hurt because you've put your faith in the wrong person."

She looked up. "You're talking about my father again."

He nodded, his gaze on the bandage that circled her wrist. "I need to warn you to take precautions. There's a possibility that other crimes could be involved. If Bocci and your adoptive father are working together—"

"No!" she said, cutting off his words. "There is no way my dad would be behind the break-in and the fire."

"Yet you accept that he could have been behind the abduction of an infant?"

"No. Yes. That's different. You said it yourself. He and my mom were desperate for a child. And they didn't intend to harm me. They loved me."

"He could be desperate to avoid charges now," Jake said. "There's no statute of limitations on kidnapping, and the U.S. has an extradition treaty with Australia."

She uncoiled from the corner of the couch and leaned forward to grab Jake's shoulders. "Would the Grossos pursue that?"

"They only want to find their daughter."

"Thank God."

"But Floyd wouldn't know that. If you are Gina, then he has valid reasons to want this investigation stopped."

She wanted to shake him, but he was too solid and barely moved. She stabbed a finger at his chest instead. "My father might have made mistakes, and he might have done something awful to the Grossos years ago, but I don't believe he would do anything criminal now."

"Becky…"

"What about the blogger? The person who put the story about Gina on the Internet? Whoever that is obviously knows about the kidnapping."

"The blogger wouldn't want to stop the truth from coming out after revealing the story in the first place."

"Then what about the other women who claimed they were Gina?" she asked quickly. "Any one of them might have resented the way you ruled them out and could be trying to get even. Or maybe there's someone else who hasn't come forward yet. They wouldn't want you to prove I'm Gina because that would ruin their chances. Did you think of that?"

"It's possible."

"So why are you fixated on blaming my father?"

"Becky, please, calm down." He took her hand from his chest and squeezed it. "I'm not fixated on anyone. I'm only trying to protect you, but I can see that I'm making a mess of explaining myself. I haven't even gotten to the main reason I came over."

"There's more?"

"You need to make sure you lock and chain your door whenever you're in this apartment. I've asked Len to send a patrol car through the neighborhood at frequent intervals. You'd better keep your phones turned on, too," he added, getting to his feet. He went to the hall to switch her phone ringer back on, then returned to stand at the end of the couch. He made no move to sit. "And until this is over, I don't want you going anywhere on your own. If you need to go out, let me know and I'll go with you."

She frowned. "Don't you think that's excessive?"

He regarded her in silence for a moment. His fingers tightened around the head of his cane. "Do you remember reading about the death of Alan Cargill?"

Becky nodded. Everyone around NASCAR had grieved when the patriarch of the Cargill team had been killed. "Tara told me about it. She was at the awards banquet when it happened."

"I've spoken with the detective handling the case. We both think there's a possibility it's related to the abduction of the Grossos' baby."

She felt a chill. "How?"

"The killer might have wanted to silence him."

"Oh, my God," she whispered, rubbing her arms.

"I'm not telling you this to upset you, Becky. It's for your protection. Regardless of who Bocci is working for, you need to be aware there could be some risk in continuing the course we've set."

"What are you saying? Do you want me to give up?"

He didn't reply right away. "Technically, I'm employed by the Grossos so it would be their call, but I don't think giving up would make you any safer. The only real solution is to get indisputable proof of who you are. Or who you aren't."

"Another DNA test."

"Yes. I've contacted Kent. He's willing to provide another sample later this week."

"Great. I'll do the same."

"We'll have to use a different lab. Len's going to arrange

it through police department channels, and this time we'll make sure there's no paper trail to follow."

She chewed her lip while she tried to process what he'd said. Finding her birth family had been her dream. Getting close to the truth should have made her happy. Instead, the whole affair was turning into a nightmare. She shoved herself off the couch and paced to the living-room window.

"Becky, are you all right?"

She looked blindly at the moonlit yard. "I just can't believe the man who raised me, the man I called father for my entire life, would do anything to hurt me."

"Not intentionally, no. But your father has a strong motive to keep the truth buried. Ralph Bocci is bad news. He's got an arrest record that stretches back to his teens and he might not follow instructions all that well."

"Someone else could have hired Bocci."

"True. There's a definite possibility another party is involved." He paused. "But it's also true that sometimes the people we love don't deserve our trust. I'd hate to see you get hurt."

There was something in his voice that caught her attention. A hint of sadness. She shifted her focus so she could see his reflection in the glass. "Who are you talking about, Jake?"

"What do you mean? We were talking about Floyd."

"I'm not so sure." She lowered the blind over the window and turned to face him. "You sounded as if you were thinking of someone else. Who let you down? Who didn't deserve your trust?"

"This has nothing to do with me."

"I think it does. I know you've got a problem with trust. You can't understand how I can trust my father, but you said you get along with your family." She narrowed her eyes. "This has to be about your engagement."

"That's old history."

"Is it?"

Jake lifted his hand impatiently. "We've already established the fact that you and I are wired differently when it comes to risk. Let's leave it at that."

"No, I'd like to know," she persisted. "Did your fiancée let you down? Did she cheat on you? Is that why you're so averse to the idea of love and trust? Because she hurt you?"

"You're only asking this because you're upset and trying to change the subject by turning it on me."

"That may be, but your personality colors everything you do, and it's skewing your view of the facts."

"I can say the same about you."

"You already have. You're making me question my faith in my father. You're ripping apart my life. Don't you think I have a right to know about yours?"

He pressed his lips together, as if he were trying to restrain himself from responding. Then he moved around the couch, placed both hands on the head of his cane and leaned toward her. "You're right about one thing, Becky. My personal feelings have been getting in the way of my judgment when it comes to this case. And it's true, I don't put much faith in love, and I do have a problem with trust." His voice roughened. "But you're wrong about my fiancée. Heather didn't cheat on me. It would have been simpler if she had."

"But she did hurt you."

"I can't tell you whether she did or not, because the day she left I was still in the hospital and too doped up with painkillers to feel much of anything."

She took an involuntary step backward, grasping the windowsill to steady herself. In spite of what he claimed, she could see the shadow of remembered pain in his eyes. "What happened, Jake?"

"We had postponed our wedding because of Desert Storm. I'd wanted to have a quick ceremony before I was deployed, but she'd been planning it ever since we'd been in high school. I didn't want to disappoint her, so we were going to get married when I got back. Then this happened," he said, whacking his cane into his bad leg.

He didn't appear to feel the blow, but Becky flinched at the violence of his gesture.

"The doctors said I'd never walk again," he continued. "Heather didn't want to be tied for life to a cripple. I'd always been the one to take care of her, and she couldn't conceive of having our roles reversed so she left."

"My God," Becky muttered. Any anger she might have been feeling toward Jake transformed to outrage on his behalf. She'd thought Jake's accident and his broken engagement had both contributed to his cautious nature. She'd never guessed the two events had been related. This was worse than she could have imagined. He'd said he'd been on painkillers, but no medication in the world would have dulled that suffering. "How could she have deserted you when you needed her most?"

"I was no longer the same man she'd agreed to marry. Obviously, she wasn't the woman I'd thought I'd known, either. She probably saved both of us from a lifetime of misery."

She moved away from the window and curled her hands around his where he gripped his cane. "I'm sorry, Jake."

"Don't be. Heather did me a favor. If it hadn't been for her, I might not have been so damned determined to prove the doctors wrong."

"But she was wrong. You were still the same man you'd always been. It was just the outside that had changed."

He shook his head. "No, Becky. I did change. I got smarter."

"You mean you got cynical."

"Take it from me. It's always better to discover the truth about someone sooner rather than later."

She lifted her hands from his and cradled his face in her

palms. The truth? It continued to develop before her eyes. In a few terse sentences, Jake had revealed a betrayal that must have sliced him to his soul. The more she learned about him, the more she realized there were other facets she had yet to discover. She'd once been impressed by the strength he'd needed to overcome the injury to his leg. That paled in comparison to the strength of character he'd needed to heal his heart.

Then again, his heart couldn't have healed entirely. That was why he was so adamant about not taking another chance with love or marriage. Heather's betrayal had left deep scars. Was it any wonder he was unwilling to lay himself open to that kind of pain again?

He clenched his jaw. "I don't want your pity, Becky."

"I don't pity you, Jake. I…" She caught her breath on the word she was about to say. She slid her hands to Jake's neck and stretched up to kiss him.

He held himself stiffly, not responding.

Becky pulled back to look at his face. "I don't pity you," she repeated. "I just want to kiss you."

"Why?"

She grasped the front of his shirt. "Honestly?"

"Yes."

"I need to touch you, Jake." She pressed her lips to the base of his throat and spoke against his skin. "I want to feel your arms around me and taste your scent on my tongue because it makes me feel like home." She nuzzled her nose beneath his chin. "And to be completely honest, it's late, we're tired and I think we've both said more than enough for tonight. I don't really want to talk anymore, do you?"

His chest rose and fell with a shuddering breath, then he clamped one arm behind her waist to lift her feet from the floor, walked to the front of the couch and pulled her down to the cushions on top of him. Even though she could feel the weariness in his body, he proceeded to give her a kiss that scorched her clear down to the soles of her feet.

For what had to be the hundredth time, Becky tried to remind herself that her feelings for Jake could be a result of the situation. Her emotions were confused. These were exceptional circumstances.

But one of these days, she was going to run out of excuses and have to put a name to what she felt.

CHAPTER NINE

CYNTHIA WAITED until the servant had left the dining room before she set her teacup in its saucer and pressed the phone to her ear. That fool Bocci. She'd given him a simple job and he'd managed to foul it up. "Where are you now?"

"That's not important."

"The police are looking for you. They've been to the plant."

There was a faint sucking noise as he drew on his cigarette. "I need money."

"What do you intend to do?"

"Maybe you should worry about that, Mrs. Brown. I might turn myself in and cut a deal."

She rose from the table and walked to the French doors that overlooked the terrace. The grounds stretched to the fence in a pleasing progression of well-tended flower beds. Early morning dew sparkled from petals and leaves. It promised to be a lovely day. Everything seemed so ordinary. How could this be happening? "That would be unwise. You have nothing to bargain with, Mr. Bocci."

"Wrong. I'll bet the cops would be real interested to hear how you want to know about the Becky Peters case. To tell you the truth, I wondered about that myself. Is she Gina Grosso or not?"

Pain gripped Cynthia's chest. She muffled the receiver against her shoulder as she hissed for air. When the ache had receded, she lifted her chin and spoke. "What an outrageous story. You've undoubtedly fabricated this as an attempt to coerce me into letting you keep your position with us."

"What?"

"I suppose this is what we deserve for giving a criminal a second chance," she said. She mentally reviewed the words she'd already spoken. What if Bocci was recording this? It was a possibility she should have considered earlier, although she doubted whether he had the brains to arrange it. "I should have had you fired the moment plant security caught you trying to leave the grounds with company property."

He coughed. "We both know why you kept me around."

"I'm afraid I have a soft heart when it comes to my employees, just like my father. I donate to numerous charities. My reputation in the community is beyond reproach. No one could possibly believe I would have any reason—"

"Cut the crap, lady. You might think I'm stupid but I remember what I read in that detective's files. Becky Peters's father used to work for Gerald. There's gotta be a connection."

"I have no idea what you're talking about," she said, struggling to keep her voice steady. "I've never heard of these Peters people."

"It's kinda late to play dumb. You're in this as deep as I am."

"Mr. Bocci—"

"Why'd you foist the kid on Peters? Did you figure he'd take the fall if anyone found out?"

Her legs started to tremble. She clutched the curtains beside the doors.

"But if you didn't want it, why did you snatch the kid in the first place, huh?" Bocci continued. "That's what I can't figure out."

She swallowed hard. "You are obviously delusional. I'm not going to listen to this any further."

"Then I'll make it short. I want fifty grand, cash, or I go to the cops. I'll call tomorrow and tell you where to bring it."

The connection was severed. Cynthia waited until her hands stopped shaking, then closed the phone and slipped it into the pocket of her suit. She continued to focus on the gardens. They were peaceful and orderly, just how she liked things. She needed to suppress her panic and put her thoughts in order, too.

Would Bocci make good on his threat? Fifty thousand dollars might make him disappear, but it wouldn't solve her problem. What would Bocci be willing to do for five times that amount? That was an avenue worth pursuing. Men like him had no scruples. Enough money could very well bury the secret for good. It's what her father should have done in the first place. She could afford it. To keep the life she had, no price would be too high.

"Hello, Cynthia."

Hank's voice broke into her thoughts. She took a moment to compose herself, then turned to watch her husband move into the room.

He was wearing the black shorts and frayed white T-shirt he insisted on using as his exercise clothes. Instead of coming to greet her properly, he crossed to the sideboard and poured himself a glass of orange juice.

"Good morning, darling," she said, moving toward the table. She decided he probably hadn't wanted to kiss her because he hadn't yet showered. "I missed you at breakfast."

"I was in the gym." Hank tipped back his head to empty the glass of juice, then set it down on the silver tray with a click. "I needed a workout. It helps me think."

She let her gaze roam over him greedily. "I don't know why you drive yourself so hard. You're in wonderful shape."

He fisted his hands on the ends of the towel that hung around his neck. "You know I don't care how I look."

She pressed her lips together. Oh, yes, she knew. Hank didn't appreciate how gifted he'd been with respect to his appearance. If not for her guidance, he would likely let himself get slovenly. She smoothed her hands over her skirt. "I'm glad you found me before I left for the office."

"Your maid told me you were in here. We need to talk."

Your maid. Even after almost thirty-one years, Hank still hadn't become comfortable with the concept that the household staff were here to wait on him. "Of course, darling," she said. "What's on your mind?"

"I keep waiting for the right time, hoping things will change, but they don't. I can't put it off any longer." He turned to face her squarely. "This isn't working, Cynthia."

"What are you talking about?"

"Us. We can't go on this way. I want a divorce."

She pressed the heel of her hand to her chest. The pain was worse than what she'd felt when she'd spoken with Bocci, even though the source wasn't physical this time. Why now? Why today? Hadn't she been given enough to deal with? "Hank, darling…"

"You must have realized this was coming, Cynthia."

"I have noticed you've been showing some tension lately. You're just overworked. Isn't the assistant I hired for you easing your load? I'll fire him and get another."

"You know it isn't about the company, it's about our marriage. You must feel the same way, since you stopped going to counseling."

The panic she'd managed to suppress only minutes ago was pushing its way back to the surface. This wasn't fair. How could he bring this up now? "Counseling wasn't necessary. We're simply having a rough patch. I realize I've been under some strain lately, and I apologize for that."

"Then why won't you share your problems with me?"

"Darling, I love you. I would never want to burden you with my problems."

"But that's what marriage should be about. Two people

share their lives as equal partners. You've been treating me
the way your father treated you, indulging me and smothering me, all in the name of love."

"If I spoil you it's because I love you. We're fine, Hank."

"No, we're not, and we haven't been for a long time. I
feel like a pet instead of a husband. We don't even share a
room anymore, Cynthia."

"That's for your sake, Hank. With Daddy's health the way
it is, I'm often called to his room in the night." She rounded
the table and held out her hands. "He's ninety-one. He won't
be around forever, and then the situation will change. Surely
you can be patient."

Hank tightened his jaw. He took her hands and squeezed
them briefly, then stepped back. "You know I love Gerald
like a father. He's been good to me."

"He loves you, too, darling. He would be devastated to
know you're not happy. He was your staunchest defender,
even after you quit his team and left him high and dry."

A spasm of pain flickered across Hank's handsome features.

Cynthia felt a moment's guilt for causing it, but her
husband was hers. She would use any means to keep him,
even if it meant reminding him what he owed her. She
stroked her fingertip down his arm. "I supported you, Hank,
during the worst years of your life. I never gave up on you.
Surely you're not saying you want to give up on us."

He looked at her. "I haven't forgotten you were there for
me after Amy died. I know I fell apart. I lost heart for everything I had loved, and if it weren't for you and your father,
I never would have gotten over my grief. My loyalty to both
of you is what made me stick it out and try for as long as I
have, but any debt I owed you was paid long ago. Our
marriage is one-sided, Cynthia. You always claim you love
me but I don't think you even know who I am anymore."

No, *no!* Hank was her husband. He couldn't be slipping

away. Not now when the nightmare was almost over. Whatever it took, whatever the cost, she wasn't going to stand by and watch her world fall apart. If Bocci wouldn't help her, she'd hire someone else who would.

She grasped Hank's forearms. She didn't realize how hard she was gripping until she saw him flinch. Her nails had sunk into his flesh. She tempered her grip and slid her hand to his cheek. "That's not true. You mean everything to me, Hank. Please, let me prove it to you. We'll take a vacation together. Daddy won't mind. Just wait until I settle the latest crisis at the plant. Will you do that?"

"What crisis?"

"It's nothing for you to worry about." She smoothed his hair into place. "Once I transfer some funds and dispose of a few minor assets, I'll have it all under control."

IT WAS ODD to see Zack Matheson's No. 548 car at rest. Its smooth contours and ground-hugging stance appeared made to be in motion, yet for the past two hours it had been parked on the pit road of the Halesboro track. Not because it needed repairs. No, it didn't have a scratch. The electric-blue finish gleamed like a mirror in the early morning sunlight. The coveralled pit crew that would normally be servicing it were puttering around the garage or lounging at a nearby picnic table. They had been temporarily replaced by a photographer, his assistant, makeup and wardrobe people and a guy in a pink shirt who called himself an art director.

Jake angled his baseball cap to shade his eyes, folded his arms over his chest and leaned one shoulder against the wall of the garage. Becky was modeling Matheson Racing's new Zack Matheson merchandise. Currently, she was wearing a snug-waisted windbreaker in the same electric-blue color as the car. The art director had positioned her half in and half out of the driver's-door window, as if she were in the process of pulling herself out. It was an eye-catching pose. Her glorious hair was caught by the breeze, framing her face in a tumble of honey-streaked curls. She turned her face toward the corner where Jake stood and flashed a smile. Even though the smile had been for the camera, it still made Jake's pulse speed up.

He didn't think he would ever get used to her beauty. At times like this, part of him continued to marvel how a woman who looked like Becky would want to be seen with a guy who looked like him. She genuinely didn't care about his appearance. She was a woman in a million.

He tore his gaze away from her and did a scan of the area. He'd been acting as her bodyguard for almost a week now. So far, he hadn't spotted any trouble, but he couldn't afford to relax his vigilance. It was an ongoing challenge to remain focused when guarding Becky was so enjoyable.

With the exception of their taste in food, they were discovering a surprising number of things they had in common. They were both architecture junkies, they both loved old Peter Sellers movies, and neither of them could care less about politics, though Becky didn't hesitate to voice her opinions on what she read in the news. He admired the way she was fearless when she felt passionately about something. And then there was the way she kissed.

Oh, yeah. That was a big part of why the past week had gone by so enjoyably. Becky could stir him up with just a smile or a look. Sometimes merely the sound of her voice made him ache to have her in his arms. So far he'd managed to restrain himself from taking advantage of their situation and spending the nights in her bed, but it was costing him. He'd gone home to so many cold showers he was surprised he hadn't come down with pneumonia.

It was getting tougher and tougher to remember they

were no longer merely dating. The reason he was spending so much time with her was to protect her. That had to remain his primary concern, no matter what his libido was telling him. Clearly, she was emotionally vulnerable, and she'd latched on to him because she needed someone to help her through a difficult time. The second set of DNA samples had been taken from Becky and Kent the previous week. Once the test result came through—whatever it proved—she was bound to reassess their relationship.

Jake had seen the pattern before. It was similar to what had happened with Heather. When situations changed, feelings did, too. He'd be smart to remember that before he got his own emotions involved any deeper.

"That's some show they're putting on there. But kind of slow for my taste."

Jake glanced at the older man who had moved to stand beside him. It was Doug Dalhousie, one of the mechanics Earl Buckley had told him about who had worked with Becky's father on the Shillington team. Jake had spoken with Doug the previous month in New Hampshire but he hadn't learned anything about Peters that Earl hadn't already covered. "'Morning, Doug. How are things going?"

"Won't know until we can get back to testing. They told us we'd get some laps in before noon. How much longer you think they'll be?"

"I've got no idea. It's hard to believe how long it takes to snap a few pictures."

The photographer pointed to a white gauze screen on a stand that was diffusing the sunlight. His assistant scurried around the car to pull the screen a few feet closer. Becky slipped out of the car window and was immediately surrounded by the makeup people. They took the windbreaker with them when they retreated, leaving her in a scoop-necked, bright blue T-shirt.

"How come you're here, anyway, Jake?" Doug asked. "Have the Grossos got you spying for them?"

He laughed. "No, Doug. I'm with her," he said, tipping his head toward Becky.

"The model? I didn't know you had a daughter."

Jake's smile froze. He'd reminded himself of the age difference often enough. Nevertheless, Doug's assumption had stung. "She's not my daughter. She's Becky Peters." He paused. "We're dating," he added, giving the simplest explanation for his presence. It was the same thing he and Becky had told everyone else who had wondered. Besides, it was partly true.

Doug gaped at him, then jabbed a bony elbow into Jake's ribs. "Good for you. Wish I had luck like that. She's a good-looking woman."

"That she is."

"Wait. What did you say her name was again?"

"Becky Peters." Jake watched Doug's face, interested in his reaction. "Floyd Peters's daughter. I was asking you about him last month."

"So she's Floyd's kid? Was that why you were asking about him, because you wanted to date her?"

"Something like that."

"Huh. Remember how I told you about Shillington's daughter and Shanks?"

Jake nodded. One of the things Doug had recalled about the summer the Grossos' baby had been abducted was how his team's driver, Hank "Shanks" Brown, had eloped with Gerald Shillington's daughter. "Yes, I do. Why?"

"There must have been more than ten years between them, only it was the other way around. She was the one who was older than him. I don't remember Floyd being bothered by it."

Had Doug brought this up as a way of making up for his previous gaffe? "That's good to know."

"Too bad Shanks quit racing after he got married. I can't recall him even showing up at a track after, either. Guess he figured he didn't need to work anymore." Doug squinted at Becky. "It's funny. Floyd's kid doesn't look like him, but she does remind me of someone."

"You probably saw Becky's face in an advertisement. A lot of people feel as if they know her."

"Maybe." Doug gave Jake another nudge with his elbow. "She looks good with that car, doesn't she? Like she was born for life on a track."

Jake returned his gaze to Becky as Doug wandered back into the garage. Zack Matheson, looking lean and dangerous in his racing uniform, joined the activity beside his car for the next series of shots. Becky seemed as much at ease with the vehicle as Zack did, and why shouldn't she? She was a NASCAR fan, and she'd grown up attending races.

Was there such a thing as inherited memory? If there was, and if she did turn out to be Dean's daughter, then her interest in the sport could have been in her genes. Heredity would explain the sense of recognition a lot of people mentioned when they saw her, too. Not that Becky had any specific features in common with either Dean or Patsy, but there could be a general family resemblance that people who knew them picked up on. Come to think of it, during all the time Jake had spent with Becky, the only people who had said she looked familiar had been directly involved with NASCAR.

The poses with Zack appeared to be the final ones. Once he left, the photographer and his assistants began gathering their gear. Becky had just finished a brief discussion with the pink-shirted art director when a man Jake didn't recognize approached her. He was too well dressed to be one of the Matheson team, but he didn't seem to belong to the crew who had been doing the modeling shoot, either.

Jake shoved away from the garage wall and moved as

quickly as he could toward Becky. She'd asked him to give her space to do her job, yet judging by her body language, she wasn't happy with whatever this new arrival was saying. Jake wasn't pleased with how close the man was standing, either. He had placed his fingers on her arm and was leaning forward, crowding her against the side of the car.

Becky had already maneuvered away from the car and was stepping back as Jake reached her side. She smiled and stretched to give him a quick kiss on the cheek, then wiped the spot with her fingertips. "Oops, sorry. I forgot about the lipstick," she murmured. "They layered it on like icing."

Jake wanted her to leave the lipstick smear right where it was as proof she'd put her mark on him. He also wanted to glare at the man who'd been touching her. Or to be more accurate, he wanted to pick up the guy by his designer collar and hurl him over the roof of Zack's car. The urge surprised him. He wasn't normally this possessive when he dated a woman. Then again, these weren't normal circumstances. He was acting as Becky's bodyguard. It was to be expected that he'd be more protective…

Ah, who was he fooling? His emotions were already so tangled up he was wasting his time trying to make excuses. He draped his free arm across Becky's shoulders, staking his claim in terms any male should understand.

"Tony Winters," the man said, thrusting his hand toward Jake. "And you are?"

Because of his cane, the only way Jake could accept Winters's hand was to let go of Becky, a fact he was sure Winters had realized. He kept the handshake brief, but he did put enough force into his grip to elicit a wince. "Jake McMasters."

"Tony is the team accountant for Matheson Racing," Becky said.

Jake had guessed from the man's soft palm that he didn't work with anything much heavier than a pencil. "What's an accountant doing at the track?"

Winters smiled, revealing a set of perfect, recently whitened teeth. "There's more to this business than racing, pops. We're going to push Zack Matheson merchandise for the rest of the season." He turned his smile back to Becky. "Thanks to our hot cover girl, our ads are bound to catch everyone's attention."

Pops? Jake was sorry now he had restrained himself from crushing the man's hand. He ignored Winters and looked at Becky. "Are you done here?"

"Almost." She retrieved her modeling bag and took out a paper form. "I still need to get my voucher signed by the client."

"I can take care of that for you," Winters said, moving forward to intercept her. He put the form on the hood of the car, scribbled his signature and returned it to Becky. "It's been a pleasure. I look forward to seeing you again, Becky. I'll have our P.R. rep call you. Perhaps we could discuss it over dinner."

"Actually, he would have to call my agent. He handles all my bookings," she said, ignoring his suggestion of dinner. She separated part of the form he'd just signed and handed it back to him. "Here's your copy of the hours worked and the rate I agreed on. I'll return this T-shirt to the wardrobe people."

"Please, keep it, Becky, with our compliments," Winters said, with an appreciative gleam in his eyes. He moved his gaze to her chest. "I can't think of a better way to promote our clothing line."

Jake eyed the height of the car roof, calculating how hard he'd need to fling Winters over it for him to land in the middle of the track.

If Becky noticed Winters's blatant ogling, she gave no

sign of it. She politely said goodbye to him, waved to the rest of the crew, then looped her bag over her shoulder and hooked her hand in Jake's elbow. He set a brisk pace as they left the track and headed for the parking lot, partly to get her away from her admirer and partly because he needed to work off some steam. Winters had some cheek, all but asking Becky on a date right in front of him. At least the guy hadn't asked him if he was Becky's father.

They were almost at his car before she spoke. "Thanks, Jake," she said.

"You're welcome, but why are you thanking me?"

"Because you let me handle the jerk my way."

"Jerk? What jerk?"

"Tony Winters. The guy you were thinking about punching."

"Me? Nah."

"Be honest. I saw the look on your face. Your cheek was twitching. It's a dead giveaway."

"Okay, I got ticked off because the guy wasn't behaving respectfully toward you. But I told you the truth—what I was thinking of doing didn't involve punching him. His teeth are too pretty. He probably would have sued me."

She laughed and released his arm so he could take his keys from his pocket. "Worse than that, he might have spread the word that I'm difficult to work with. At my age, I need all the jobs I can get."

"*Your* age?"

"I think I told you about that. I don't have many productive years left to build my savings." She paused as he opened the passenger door for her. "Not that I'd be willing to put up with a client who made advances, but what Tony Winters did back there was really pretty mild."

Jake waited until she slid inside the car, then closed her door and went around to the other side. He started the engine and turned on the air-conditioning full blast before he twisted to look at her. Considering the age gap between them, it was bizarre that Becky would have any reason to worry about *her* age, but he did understand her concern. "Does that happen a lot? I mean guys coming on to you when you're working."

"Not as often as you might think. Most people in the fashion industry are only interested in getting the job over with. They've seen too many models to get impressed by appearances."

"But you do get propositioned."

"Sure. It's an occupational hazard of making money with my looks. Some men assume that's all there is to me." She set her bag on the floor between her feet and rummaged around inside it. She came up with a pot of face cream and a bag of cotton pads. "I hope you don't mind if I do this while we drive," she said, applying the cream to her face. "It's not good for my skin to leave on this much heavy makeup in warm weather, but I didn't want to hang around the set any longer."

"No problem," he said, putting the car into gear. A few other vehicles, probably belonging to people from the fashion shoot, were already heading toward the parking lot exit. He waited for them to pass, then eased onto the road, accelerating slowly so he wouldn't jar Becky while she continued her task.

He was pleased she felt comfortable enough around him to do something as personal as removing her makeup. Yet again, he marveled at how completely without vanity she was. She treated her appearance as matter-of-factly as he treated his surveillance gear. Both were necessary assets for their businesses. On the other hand, storing his camera in his equipment cabinet at the end of a stakeout wasn't anywhere near as intimate as what Becky was doing. He inhaled slowly as the scent of her cream drifted toward him. "Gardenias."

"Mmm?"

"I noticed that scent when we first met. It suits you."

"Really?" Her voice was muffled as she dragged a cotton pad over her mouth, wiping away what was left of the layers of lipstick and gloss.

"It's sweet. It makes me think of warm nights and soft skin."

She rubbed cream over her forehead. "And that's what you thought of when we first met?"

"Not exactly." He looked at her as he slowed for an amber light. "That day in the park when you called my name I thought I knew you. I realized later it was because I'd seen your picture."

She skimmed a pad with some kind of liquid over her face, shoved the paraphernalia back into her modeling bag, then pulled out a lacy elastic and fiddled with it between her fingers. "Tingles," she said. "That's what I felt when you touched my hand the first time."

He smiled as he remembered. "For me, it was more like tickles. As if I was standing too close to a high-voltage wire."

Her movements were slow as she gathered her hair off her neck and corralled it into a loose knot on the top of her head. "But I felt as if I knew you, too, Jake." She hooked her knee on the seat and twisted to face him. "I felt as if we were connected somehow. What do you think that meant?"

The light was still red, so he lifted his hand from the wheel and stroked her cheek. Her freshly cleaned skin was like warm satin beneath his fingers. He tried to focus on the pleasure of touching her rather than think about her question, yet he knew the answer anyway. "You probably felt gratitude. You knew who I was, and you realized I could be your ticket to finding your birth family."

"That's what I told myself at first, but I'm not sure about it anymore. Maybe my gut recognized that you were someone I was meant to be with. I enjoy the time we spend together, no matter what we're doing." She smiled and tilted her face toward his hand. "I think we might have been fated to meet, regardless of the circumstances. Otherwise, how do you explain those tickles you felt when you met me?"

He traced the edge of her jaw, the curve of her cheek, the thin skin at her temple, all so familiar to him now that he couldn't imagine getting through a day without her. Could there have been more to the recognition he'd felt when they'd met? He'd never felt this close to a woman after such a short time. He'd known Heather since grade school and even before they'd reached their teens he'd decided they would get married someday. He'd thought they had been fated to be together…

Sure, and look how that had turned out.

Becky had made clear what she wanted for her future weeks ago. She might talk about building her savings so that she could open her own business, but he hadn't forgotten the rest of what she'd told him that morning in the garage loft. A family. Marriage and children. He knew her well enough by now to understand how important those things were to her. He was going to try his damnedest to find her birth family for her, but that was all.

Jake returned his hand to the wheel. Becky would be better off with a man closer to her age, someone who was planning to settle down. But not like that jerk, Tony Winters. Or one of those too-pretty-to-be-true male models Jake had seen at some of her other fashion shoots. Or flashy, virility-in-a-uniform guys who drove race cars. Actually, the mere idea of any other man touching her made Jake want to break something.

Someone honked from behind them. He noticed the traffic light had turned green and stepped on the gas.

"Jake?" Becky asked.

He realized she was still waiting for an answer. He gave

her what he hoped was a casual smile. "I'd be willing to bet you give most men a high-voltage jolt when they first meet you. I got the jolt on an empty stomach, so you could say it was a gut reaction in my case, too."

She didn't respond.

He glanced at her as they entered the intersection. He could see that his flip answer had disappointed her, but it was best for both of them not to let this relationship get serious. Otherwise, someone would get hurt.

Jake glimpsed a blur of movement through the window beyond her and shifted his focus.

A green van was hurtling past the row of cars that were stopped on the cross street for the red light. It was heading straight for them.

Jake reacted instinctively and jammed the gas pedal to the floor. "Hang on!"

She was thrown back against the seat as the car jumped forward. The van roared into the spot where she had been a heartbeat earlier. It missed the passenger door, but Jake couldn't accelerate fast enough to avoid the collision entirely. The van clipped the car's back bumper as it passed by, spinning them around. Jake yanked the wheel and fought to regain control but it was no use. The car skidded across the pavement. It didn't stop until it slammed nose-first into a light pole.

CHAPTER TEN

BECKY CURLED her fingers around her soda. Her hand was shaking so badly the ice cubes rattled against the glass. She took a quick sip and set it down. "My adoptive father had nothing to do with that hit-and-run."

Jake nodded, picked up a French fry and dunked it in the puddle of gravy on his plate. He had already worked his way through a hamburger and was making inroads on his plate of fries, but Becky hadn't been able to stomach the idea of food. "I agree with her, Len," Jake said. "This was more than a cover-up or collateral damage. It was a deliberate attempt to hurt Becky. I can't see Floyd Peters going that far to protect himself. There must be a third party involved."

Becky transferred her gaze to Lieutenant Denning, who sat on the other side of the table. They had agreed to meet at Edna's, the small diner near Jake's office, so they could have dinner while they talked. Their booth provided a good amount of privacy. It was at the end of the diner farthest from the door and the cash register, and there was only a scattering of other customers, none of whom would be able to overhear their conversation over the country music that played from the speakers on the wall.

At least Jake had come around to her point of view about her father. It wasn't because he was willing to trust her feelings, though. No, he wasn't about to change that much. He put his faith in logic.

Len set down his half-eaten turkey sandwich, wiped his fingers on a paper napkin and leafed through his notebook. "I called Lucas Haines in New York before I left the office. He still hasn't found anything solid to support a link between Alan Cargill's death and the Gina Grosso case."

Jake sprinkled more salt on his fries. "That doesn't mean there isn't one."

"It's also possible that you embarked on a wild-goose chase. I think you got paranoid after the break-in last week and you're seeing conspiracies where there aren't any." Len eyed Jake's plate. "I can't believe you're still breathing. You've got more than a day's worth of sodium there."

"Yum, just the way I like it. Did you learn anything more about the van?"

Len flipped a page. "A van matching the description of the one that hit you this morning was found abandoned at a rest stop a couple of miles down the highway from Halesboro. No prints. It had been reported stolen in Concord yesterday."

Becky let go of her glass before she spilled it and tightened her fingers into a fist. The collision had happened more than eight hours ago. The police had arrived on the scene within minutes, as had a tow truck. By the time the intersection was cleaned up, Jake had contacted his insurance agent and arranged for a rental car. Everything was over, but she still found herself shaking at odd times. It was like the reaction that had plagued her after the attack at Jake's office.

Without warning, her vision filled with an image of Jake's car as she'd last seen it, dangling from the tow truck hook, its front end crumpled, its rear bumper torn off. It was a miracle that neither she nor Jake had been hurt. Aside from a few bruises from the seat belts, they'd both escaped unscathed. If it hadn't been for his quick reflexes and the sedan's air bags...

Jake laid his hand over her fist. "We can finish this later."

She shook her head. "I don't need to be coddled. I want to get to the bottom of what happened as much as you do."

He squeezed gently but didn't release her hand. "Okay, but anytime you want to go home, just say the word."

His concern brought a lump to her throat. Since they'd crawled out of the car, Jake had remained glued to her side. Under other circumstances, she would have enjoyed his attention, but he'd made it clear he was sticking with her to protect her. Although he still found reasons to touch her, and he was as solicitous as ever, it didn't feel the same. It was as if he were subtly withdrawing from her. She suspected he blamed himself for not being alert enough to spot the van sooner and avoid the collision. He felt responsible because he'd been distracted.

It was true, and she knew what had distracted him. They'd been talking about their feelings. Or at least, she'd been attempting to, but he'd deflected the conversation. She'd told him how she felt and he'd responded with a wisecrack. And now he had the perfect excuse to continue to dodge the subject.

Becky slipped her hand from Jake's and dropped it to her lap, impatient with the direction of her thoughts. This was hardly the time to worry about their relationship. She understood why Jake was so reluctant to admit there could be something special between them. The scars on his heart were as real as those scars on his leg. After what he'd gone through, it was a wonder he'd been able to open up to Becky as much as he had.

And she had no cause to find fault with him for being protective. Their safety ought to take precedence over their relationship. That mattered more than how good this past week with him had been. Or how important he was becoming to her. Or how much she cared about him. She was probably dwelling on their interrupted conversation because she didn't want to think about the nightmarish seconds that had followed it. It seemed that Jake wasn't the only one who preferred to avoid an uncomfortable topic.

She looked at Len. "What else did you find out?"

He glanced from her to Jake. "According to the uniforms who attended the scene, there were plenty of witnesses to the accident but the descriptions of the driver are all over the place. The only thing everyone agreed on was that he was male."

"It was probably Bocci," Jake said.

"The Halesboro cops are going on the theory it was just some hopped-up car thief who ran the light."

Jake grunted. "Do you believe that, Len?"

"I believe the evidence, and in this case there isn't any to indicate this was anything other than a random, hit-and-run accident." He closed his notebook and stored it in his jacket, then slid to the edge of the bench seat. "Thanks for the sandwich, but I need to get home. Nancy's got her ceramics class tonight and I promised I'd watch the kids."

"You'll let me know if you learn anything, right?" Jake asked.

"If I think it's relevant, sure."

"C'mon, Len. This is no time to start holding out on me."

"As a cop, I don't need to tell you anything." Len got to his feet. "But as your friend, I'll give you some advice. Go home and get some sleep. You look like hell." He turned and headed for the exit.

Jake rubbed his chin. His end-of-the-day beard stubble rasped beneath his palm. He glanced at Becky. "I should have had him pay for his own sandwich."

"Do you think what happened today *could* have been an accident? We could be overreacting."

"It's possible. I'd prefer to play it safe, though. Until we learn more, that's all we can do."

She thought about that for a moment, then slowly shook her head. "No, there's something else we haven't tried."

"What?"

She twisted to reach into the bag she'd left on the seat beside her and took out her phone. She flipped it open and scrolled through her directory.

"What are you doing?" Jake asked, covering her hand with his to halt her.

She checked the clock on the wall over the cash register and calculated that it would be midmorning in Melbourne. "I'm phoning my father."

Jake frowned. "Are you sure you're up to it?"

No, she wasn't sure. Her stomach was curling into a hard knot at the idea. In spite of her ongoing defense of her father, she dreaded the idea of a confrontation. She'd had some nerve for being critical of Jake because he preferred to avoid touchy subjects. She'd done that with her father for years. "This is long overdue. He deserves the chance to tell his side of the story."

"He never has before. He stonewalled me as much as he did you."

"That's true, but I was never almost killed before. He needs to know what's going on."

Jake studied her face, then released her hand. "You have a point. Floyd's bound to be more cooperative if he learns the situation has escalated."

Becky put the phone to her ear. There was a delay and a series of clicks before the number started ringing. It had been weeks since she'd spoken with him. Although she was expecting it, she still felt a jolt when she heard her father's voice.

She hesitated while she debated what to say. Should she come right out and ask him whether or not he and her mother stole an infant girl from her parents thirty-one years ago? Ask him if he knew who would want to run down his adoptive daughter? This was why she hadn't called him earlier. It felt disloyal to question him. She didn't want to hurt him.

Or had she only been protecting herself from getting an answer she hadn't wanted to hear? She glanced around the diner. Only a handful of customers were left. The background music was still providing privacy, but maybe she should have waited until she got home. Then again, she would probably find some other reason to put off this conversation once she got there.

"Becky? Is that you?"

She could delay no longer. He'd obviously recognized her number. "Hi, Dad."

"Is something wrong?"

She closed her eyes. He sounded just the way he always had. Even though they were no longer as close as they'd been when she'd been a child, he could still tell when she was upset. "I was in an accident today."

"How bad was it? Are you okay? Were you hurt?"

"I'm fine."

"What happened?"

"It was a hit-and-run. I was in Jake McMasters's car. He called you last month, remember?"

"The detective. Yes, I remember. Are you sure you're all right? Where are you? Are you in a hospital?"

"We didn't need to go." She blinked hard and focused on Jake's face. "We're both fine. The paramedics checked us out already."

"Thank God." There was a pause. "What were you doing with McMasters? You're not still looking into your adoption, are you, Becky? You know how I feel about that. You need to leave it alone."

He sounded so anxious, she had to restrain herself from apologizing. "I can't stop, Dad."

"Of course, you can. Weren't your mother and I enough for you? Why are you do determined to find another family?"

It was the same thing she'd heard since she'd discovered she was adopted. The guilt it stirred was the same, too. She fought the urge to back down. "I won't be safe until I find out the truth."

"*Safe?* What do you mean? What's going on there?"

His response had been loud enough for Jake to hear. He leaned closer to Becky and motioned for her to tip the phone so that he could listen.

Becky hesitated briefly before she complied. "Someone's trying to stop Jake's investigation," she said. "A man attacked us with a knife."

"Oh, Becky! You weren't hurt, were you?"

"No. Jake protected me," she said. "There was also a fire at the lab that was running the DNA test."

"What DNA test?"

"To see whether or not I'm Gina Grosso."

Silence.

"Dad?"

"Becky, I told you to leave this alone. Nothing good can come of it."

"I can't stop now." She took a deep breath to steady herself, then blurted out the question she really wanted to ask. "Dad, *am* I Gina Grosso?"

"Becky…"

"I need to know, Dad. I deserve to know. All these years you've been worried that our relationship won't be the same if you tell me who I am, but it's the other way around. Things won't be the same if you *don't* tell me."

"I'm sorry, Becky."

"I'm sorry, too, Dad. I'm sorry it's come to this. I'd like to hear it from you, but either way I'm going to learn the truth. Because if you don't tell me, the DNA test will."

The silence stretched out longer this time. Becky steeled herself against a denial or another demand to drop the issue of her parentage.

His reply, when it came, wasn't what she'd expected. "Becky," he said slowly, "I don't honestly know who you are."

"What?"

"Your mother and I were afraid to ask."

"I don't understand. How could you not know?"

"You came to us only two weeks after the Grosso baby disappeared. We had our suspicions, but we wanted you so much, we didn't care who you were born to. Mom and I loved you as soon as we saw you. I swear to you, Becky, from that day forward I've thought of you as *my* child. You'll always be my baby, no matter what that DNA test shows."

Tears blurred her vision. She blinked them back, trying to grasp what her father was saying. "You didn't take me from the hospital nursery?"

"God, no! We wouldn't do that! It was a private adoption. It's only the timing of it that made us wonder if you were Gina. No one gave us any hint that you were."

"So you really don't know who I am?"

"I swear to you, Becky. I never knew. I never asked."

"Why?"

"Because I didn't want to lose you."

Jake grasped her hand and spoke into the phone. "Mr. Peters, this is Jake McMasters."

"Yes?" he said, his tone hardening.

"Becky may not have made this clear enough to you, so I will. Your daughter is in danger. Someone is trying to stop us from learning the truth about her origins."

"If Becky's in danger, it's because of you, McMasters. I can't believe it's got anything to do with her adoption."

"If she's Gina—"

"No. I told you, we only wondered about it, same as she's wondering about it now. That doesn't mean it's true."

"Then who arranged the adoption?"

"A man I knew asked for my help. He said his teenage cousin had a baby and the family wanted it kept private."

"Who was he?"

"He was a good man. He gave me a break when no one else would. He knew how much my wife and I wanted a child. I owe him for that. I swore not to say anything."

"I don't give a damn what you promised, Floyd. If you love your daughter as much as you claim to, you should stop thinking about yourself for a change and think of her."

"I always think of her. Becky is the most important—"

"Then prove it. Prove that your daughter's faith in you is justified and tell me who gave you the baby."

There was a pause. Jake waited him out. Finally, Floyd muttered a curse under his breath and spoke. "It was my old boss. Gerald Shillington."

IT WAS A NASCAR Sprint Cup Series race weekend in Indianapolis. Jake had planned to attend it with Becky, so their plane tickets and motel rooms had been booked more than a week ago. That was fortunate, because by Saturday there wouldn't be a vacancy in the area. They had arranged to arrive a day early in order to catch a few of the practice runs. Instead, they were miles from the track and neither one was thinking about the upcoming race. Another far more serious purpose had been added to their trip.

Jake steered the rental car past a pair of stone gateposts and started up the long driveway toward the Shillington house. Like the other homes in this upscale Indianapolis suburb, it was set well back from the road. The three-story Tudor had dark wood beams crisscrossing its gleaming white stucco and diamond-paned windows that glinted

golden in the afternoon sun. It sat amid at least five acres of
lush lawns, formal flower beds and meticulously squared-
off yew hedges. There was no sign of dogs running loose or
kids riding tricycles in this neighborhood.

The address had been easy to obtain, since Gerald
Shillington had lived in the same place for more than sixty
years. He was in his nineties now and in fragile health, so
apart from rare excursions to his suite at the Indianapolis
racetrack, he seldom left the property.

Yes, finding Floyd's former boss had been the easy part.
Getting to see him was another matter. Each time Jake had
called, the staff had put him off, claiming Gerald wasn't at
home. The only person who had agreed to meet with him
was Gerald's daughter, Cynthia.

Jake shifted his gaze to Becky, who was twisting her
hands in her lap. At first he'd tried to convince her to wait
for him at their motel, but she had insisted on accompanying him. He knew that if he hadn't agreed, she would have
come on her own, yet he hated to see her so tense. Still, her
honesty about her emotions was one of the things he liked
most about her.

She was bearing up well, considering the bombshell her
father had dropped. If Gerald Shillington really had given the
infant Becky to Floyd, then her dream of being Gina Grosso
likely wasn't going to come true. The scenario no longer made
sense. What possible reason could Gerald have had to steal a
baby from a hospital nursery in the first place? He hadn't been
desperate to have a child; he'd been a sixty-year-old widower
with an adult daughter. It was doubtful he would have had the
means to sneak into a Nashville nursery, either. And why
would anyone take such a risk only to give the baby away?

Trying to arrange a private adoption on behalf of a young
cousin was a more plausible scenario. A family as wealthy and
influential as the Shillingtons might have wanted to hush up

an illegitimate birth. Sure, the timing of the adoption did raise suspicions, yet sometimes coincidences really did happen.

Coincidences like a break-in and a fire, plus a hit-and-run? *If Becky's in danger, it's because of you, McMasters.*

Jake flinched as he remembered Floyd's words. He didn't want to believe them. He'd gone over his recent cases again, and he still couldn't see any reason other than the Grosso case for someone to target him. Len continued to maintain that Jake was being paranoid about the danger to Becky. Whether it was true or not didn't matter, because Jake wasn't planning to relax his vigilance.

In that sense, it was good to have Becky nearby so that he could keep an eye on her. If he'd come without her, he likely would have worried about her the whole time they were apart. Bringing her to the Shillington house wasn't much of a risk. By all reports, Gerald himself was too frail to pose a personal threat, and if he was behind the recent incidents, it was highly unlikely he would order a move against them while they were visiting him.

Yet there was another reason why Jake hadn't tried all that hard to dissuade Becky from accompanying him. One way or another, this case was going to be over soon and she would no longer need him. He wanted to enjoy her presence as long as he could.

He parked beside a marble fountain in the center of the cobblestone courtyard that led to the front entrance, then reached over to squeeze Becky's hands. "You don't need to do this," he said. "It's only a matter of time before the results of the second test come in."

"Sure, but what if something else goes wrong to delay it? Gerald Shillington has to know who I am. You don't honestly expect me to sit back and wait for a lab to call, do you?"

No, he didn't. Especially since the DNA test probably wouldn't give her the answer she hoped for.

A maid met them at the door and showed them into an elegant sitting room done in pale blue and peach. Jake suspected one of the spindly-looking side tables alone was worth more than he made in a year.

Ten minutes later, Cynthia Shillington Brown swept into the room. She was as elegant as her house, from the tasteful string of pearls at her throat to her ivory silk suit. Jake knew she had to be in her midsixties, yet her hair was jet-black and there were no signs of age on her porcelain-smooth face. Not much trace of expression, either, until she spotted Becky.

Her steps faltered. For a split second, her entire body seemed to recoil. Her eyes flashed with something that looked like recognition. She recovered quickly and extended her hand to Jake. "Mr. McMasters, I wasn't aware you were bringing someone else."

He took a moment to scrutinize her as he shook her hand. Her features had smoothed back into porcelain, yet in spite of her composed smile, her fingers were cold and less than steady. "This is Becky Peters, a friend of mine from Charlotte."

"I see." Cynthia didn't offer to shake hands with Becky. Instead she returned to the doorway and quickly slid a pair of pocket doors closed. She waved them toward a grouping of chairs near an empty fireplace, choosing a wing chair for herself. "I would offer you some refreshments but I'm afraid I must leave for an appointment shortly. How can I help you?"

"We'll try not to take up much of your time," Jake said. He waited until Becky sat, then lowered himself to the chair beside hers. "What we'd really like is to speak with your father."

"I'm sorry. As I told you on the phone, it's not possible. He isn't in good health."

"We understand that and we wouldn't stay long," Becky said. "We just need to ask him a few questions."

"You must be aware that I have taken over his position at the company," Cynthia replied, straightening the cuffs of her jacket sleeves. "Anything you need to know, you could ask me."

"It's not business," Jake said. He stacked his hands on his cane and leaned forward. "It's a personal matter."

"My father used to work for him on his NASCAR team," Becky explained. "His name is Floyd Peters."

"The Shillington team was disbanded decades ago, Ms. Peters. Although I appreciate your interest, I doubt whether my father would remember every one of his employees."

Something was off here, Jake thought. After her initial shocked reaction, Cynthia was avoiding looking at Becky altogether. And why had she bothered to close the doors if she had planned to keep their meeting brief? He felt his curiosity stir. "Perhaps you would remember him, Mrs. Brown."

Cynthia laughed delicately as she turned toward him. "I think not, Mr. McMasters. I had very little to do with my father's NASCAR phase. I was too busy with the company."

"You must have followed racing to some extent. You married the Shillington team's principal driver."

Her smile had been artificial to begin with. It disappeared altogether. "My husband lost interest in racing many years ago."

"That's a shame," Jake said. "I understood that Shanks had a lot of potential."

"Oh, I'd almost forgotten that horrid nickname."

"He would have known Becky's father, too."

"Possibly." Cynthia fingered her pearls. "I really couldn't say. Now, if you'll excuse me…"

"Mrs. Brown," Becky said quickly. "Do you know anything about a private adoption your father arranged thirty-one years ago?"

"Adoption? Heavens, no. My father wouldn't have been involved in anything of the sort. Is that what you wished to speak with him about?"

"It's really important," Becky said.

"Well, if you think to find information here, you're obviously misguided."

"Since we can't see Gerald, maybe some other member of your family could help us," Jake said. "Could we speak with your husband, Mrs. Brown? As I said, he might remember Floyd Peters."

"My husband is currently away on business." Cynthia stood abruptly and walked to the doorway. She slid the doors open. "Now, if you'll excuse me, I must leave for my appointment."

Jake took his business card from his pocket and laid it on the nearest table as he rose to his feet. "I'll leave my number with you in case you think of something that might help us."

"I doubt I will," Cynthia said. "Good day, Mr. McMasters, Ms. Peters. The maid will show you out."

Jake put his free hand on the small of Becky's back as they returned to the car. He could feel her frustration in the stiffness of her stride, but short of forcing their way through the house to find Gerald, there was nothing more they could do here.

Still, the visit hadn't been a total loss. Cynthia had obviously been nervous about something even before Becky had brought up the topic of the adoption. Yet she hadn't seemed surprised by Becky's question. That was odd. So was her reluctance to look at Becky. She'd practically given them the bum's rush when he'd mentioned talking to her husband.

Now all he had to do was figure out why.

CYNTHIA PICKED UP the business card the detective had left, ripped it into quarters and slipped the pieces into her jacket pocket. The girl had been here, in her home. No longer a looming problem or an unpleasant memory but a presence as solid as the Hepplewhite side chair she'd been sitting on. How could this be happening?

It had been like seeing a ghost. The resemblance had been uncanny. If she had been a few inches shorter, and if her hair hadn't been streaked with blond, the Peters girl would be the spitting image of her mother the year she'd been born. And she'd been right here where anyone could have seen her. Where Hank could have walked in at any time and met her. One look and he would know. He would ask questions. He would find out…

No, Hank wouldn't have walked in, Cynthia reminded herself. He'd moved into a hotel. He'd left behind every suit she'd bought him, all his tailored shirts and custom-made shoes and had taken only what he'd been able to stuff into his old suitcase. His goodbye to Gerald had been longer than his goodbye to her.

But he'd be back. Once this business with the Peters girl was over, everything would return to the way it used to be. Cynthia couldn't conceive of a life without Hank. It was impossible. He was *hers.*

She curled her fingers until she felt her nails bite into her palms. She welcomed the pain. It steadied her. She couldn't allow herself to panic.

Yet how much longer could she hold on? She hadn't heard from Bocci for almost a week. He had promised he was going to eliminate Becky Peters. She'd even paid him the first installment of the money they'd agreed upon. Obviously he'd lied, and now he wasn't returning her calls. What if McMasters managed to contact Hank? What if he brought the girl to their meeting?

Cynthia could no longer count on her husband's loyalty to blind him to the truth. He wouldn't understand her the way her father did. He wouldn't forgive what she had done to keep him. Neither would the law.

She left the sitting room, walked down the hall to her father's study and went straight to the painting that hung on the wall. It was a portrait of herself, done shortly after her college graduation. Before she'd met Hank and fallen in love. Before all of this had started. She grasped the edge of the frame, swung it away from the wall and opened the safe that was concealed behind it.

This was all Daddy's fault, she decided. She shouldn't have counted on him to begin with. It had been a mistake to rely on Bocci, too. She had run out of options. Her only choice now was to deal with the matter herself.

Cynthia reached into the safe, bypassed the remaining stack of banknotes that would have gone to paying Bocci… and wrapped her fingers around the butt of Gerald's gun.

CHAPTER ELEVEN

THE ROADHOUSE was on the highway amid a string of motels only a few miles from the Indianapolis racetrack. On a raised platform opposite the bar, a local band was doing covers of Garth Brooks songs while a digital readout over the stage displayed a countdown to the start of the next day's NASCAR Sprint Cup Series race. Becky knew the place well. She, Tara and Nicole had made it a tradition to come here whenever they were in town. The majority of the crowd who packed the round wooden tables were NASCAR fans. Most displayed their loyalties through the gear they were wearing—Becky wasn't the only one with a blue-and-white Kent Grosso shirt.

Becky likely wasn't the only one who had fantasized that she was Gina Grosso, either.

"Hey, are you all right?"

At Jake's voice, she forced a smile. The volume of the music and the chatter from the other customers made conversation difficult. She was grateful for that. She didn't share the party mood of the rest of the crowd. She picked at the label on her beer bottle with her fingernail. It wasn't even a light beer, but she wasn't in the mood to worry about calories tonight, either. "I wish you'd stop asking me that."

"What?"

"If I'm all right. It's race day tomorrow. Kent's going to blow the competition away. And as a bonus, no one's tried to T-bone us at a stoplight or to stab us lately. What more could I want?"

Jake hitched his chair closer and put his arm around her shoulders. He brought his mouth next to her ear. "I'm sorry, Becky. I'm worried about you, that's all."

She could feel his breath stir her hair. She had a sudden urge to crawl into his lap and press her face to his neck. She knew he wouldn't hesitate to comfort her, just as he always tried to protect her. That was his nature. She took another swallow of beer instead.

Jake had been nothing but considerate since they'd left the Shillington house. Even before that, he'd been treating her as if she were something fragile. She knew why. He no longer believed she was Gina and was doing his best to cushion the blow.

He might be right. Gerald Shillington would have had no motive to steal the Grossos' baby. All he would have cared about would have been his team.

She set her bottle on the table with a clunk, struck by a sudden idea. "Jake, maybe Gerald took Gina so that Dean would lose."

"I don't follow you."

She turned her head and pulled back to look at him. "Dean Grosso suspended his season to look for Gina. He didn't race for months after she was abducted. What if Gerald had been deliberately trying to knock out his competition?"

"Dean was just starting his career at the time. He was a good driver, but he wasn't a serious contender for a championship. And kidnapping a baby is a pretty extreme way to sabotage a few races."

"Maybe his daughter did it. She was in love with their team's driver. She might have thought she was helping him. People can do crazy things for love."

Jake frowned. "That's still far-fetched. Shanks quit before the end of the season anyway."

"Yes, and he married Cynthia Shillington. Don't you think that's strange? She seemed to have no interest in NASCAR at all."

"Everything about that woman was strange, including her reaction to you."

Becky chewed her lip. She had taken an instant dislike to Cynthia Shillington Brown. It wasn't merely because the woman had refused to allow them to see Gerald and had barely acknowledged Becky's presence. No, the response had gone deeper than that. When Cynthia had walked into the room, during that one instant of eye contact between them, Becky had felt a prickle of something akin to fear.

It hadn't made sense. Then again, nothing about this situation was making sense unless she was willing to believe that Gerald had told her father the truth.

"There's another possibility," Jake said.

His gaze was brimming with sympathy again. Becky didn't think she was going to like what was coming. "What?"

"The baby Gerald gave to your father might not have been a cousin's," Jake said. "It might have been his daughter's."

She jerked backward. "No way! That woman can't be my mother."

"You have to agree that she appeared nervous. She didn't seem surprised when you mentioned the adoption, either."

"That's true, but it couldn't be because I'm *hers*. Why would she give away her baby? She was getting married anyway. If they were worried about scandal all they needed to do was move up the wedding."

"Not if you weren't Hank's child."

Becky rubbed her arms. "No, she's not my mother. I won't believe it."

Jake stroked her hand. "I'll check into the Shillington

family while we're in town. There must be someone who is willing to talk to us. Gerald couldn't be the only one who knows the truth."

A woman laughed from the neighboring table. Becky looked at the group and felt a pang of envy. There were six people crowded around the table, and most of them were wearing Sanford Racing colors. They were talking together as if they were all old friends, but they could just as easily have met only minutes before. Being fellow NASCAR fans made them like family.

Becky knew that was one of the reasons she attended every race she could. She was guaranteed to feel part of the group, whatever city she happened to be in. She'd always wished to belong to a large, happy family...

"Careful what you wish for," she said.

Jake squeezed her shoulders. "What brought that on?" he asked.

"I used to wish I had a family like the Daltons. Then I wished that the Grossos were my family. I don't know whether I'd want to belong to the Shillingtons."

"Do you want me to stop, Becky?"

"Stop?"

"We don't have to keep looking for your birth parents."

"You told me it's not up to me. You're being paid by the Grossos."

He hesitated. "My job for the Grossos only entails finding out whether you're Gina. I'm offering to keep looking even if it turns out you're not."

"And you think I'm not."

He didn't reply. The regret on his face was enough of an answer. He stood and held out his hand. "It's been a long day, Becky. Let's get out of here."

Well, she couldn't say that he hadn't warned her about getting her hopes up. She grabbed her beer and drained it before she got to her feet. She wished she could pretend that her tears were from swallowing too fast.

Someone jostled her shoulder as they moved toward the exit. It was a middle-aged man with a Will Branch ball cap pulled low over a fringe of red hair. "Sorry," he said, shouting over the noise of the music. "I didn't... Hey, don't I know you?"

Becky shook her head and kept going. She wasn't in the mood to explain who she was. The posters for the blue jeans campaign and her modeling career were the last things she wanted to think about. On the other hand, there wasn't anything else she wanted to think about, either. Her dream of being Gina was over. Tara had once told her that she'd be the same person, whatever her last name turned out to be, but it wasn't that simple. If her last name was Shillington...

She could never belong in that fancy house, or get accustomed to maids, or be comfortable in pearls and silk suits. Not that she'd be welcomed there anyway, since she'd been discarded at birth as an embarrassment to the family. No one had been trying to find her. It wasn't anything like her fantasy. She closed her eyes and dropped her head back against the car seat as Jake drove to their motel.

He parked close to the staircase that led to the second floor where their rooms were and walked her to her door. "Let me check things out before you go inside," he said, taking her key from her hand.

Becky watched him from the doorway as he moved around the room. The place wasn't luxurious but as motels went it was clean and neat, with a sturdy wooden dresser and a television against one wall and a bed against another. It was easy to see that no one was lurking in the corners or the bathroom. Everything appeared to be exactly as she had left it. "Len was probably right," she said. "We must have overreacted to that break-in and the accident. They could be totally unrelated. If I'm just a teenage girl's unwanted baby, I don't think anyone's after us."

"We don't know that for sure yet," Jake said, closing the curtains on the window. "We've only started investigating the Shillingtons. It's better to be careful."

She crossed her arms, rubbing her palms over her sleeves. "I've lost count of the number of times you've said that. You've been trying to protect me from the time we met."

He turned to face her. "I tried to keep you safe."

"Right. Safe from getting my hopes up and safe from crazy ex-cons who might or might not be trying to do me harm." She laughed without humor. "You even tried to keep me safe from you."

"I realize my attitude frustrates you at times but I don't want you to get hurt. Is that so hard for you to understand?"

She shook her head. "No, it's not. I know that's how you're wired. You can't help being protective. But do you think you could knock it off? At least for tonight?"

"Becky…"

She stepped over the threshold and shut the door behind her. "Jake, I don't need you to check my locks or look under the bed for intruders. I need you to hold me."

He closed the distance between them in three strides, dropped his cane to the floor and pulled her into his arms.

Becky laid her cheek on his shoulder and pressed her face to his neck, inhaling his scent. As it always did, the feel of his embrace steadied her. "I don't want you to look for my family anymore," she mumbled. "It doesn't really matter who gave birth to me. It was all just a stupid dream."

"Give it some time." He stroked his hand over her hair. "You're disappointed now but you might feel differently about it tomorrow."

"I don't think so. My dream was about more than finding my birth family. I was looking for somewhere to belong, for someone to love me. I don't expect to find that with the Shillingtons."

"It's too soon to know that." He brushed his lips over her forehead. "Don't give up. As I've said before, you're a courageous woman, Becky."

"No, I'm not. I'm a fraud."

"Where did that come from? You're one of the most honest people I've known."

"I'm a fraud," she repeated. "People always tell me I'm beautiful. On the outside I must be, because I make my living from my looks. But there's got to be something inside me that's wrong. That's repulsive. That makes people not want me."

"No, Becky. There are all kinds of reasons people decide to give up a child for adoption."

She locked her hands behind his neck and arched back to look at his face. "Do you think that's all I'm talking about?"

"What do you mean?"

"Do *you* want me, Jake?"

A tremor went through his body. Although he'd discarded his cane, he was leaning against the door for support, so she didn't believe the tremor was from weariness. He moved his hands to her waist. "You're upset," he began.

"And you're avoiding the question." She stepped between his feet to nestle closer. "Don't run away from it this time, Jake. Don't make a joke or pretend there's nothing special between us. It seems as if you want me. Whenever we kiss, you make me feel as if we're the only two people in the world, but whenever I try to talk about it, you push me away."

"I do want you, Becky. More than you can imagine." He pulled her hard against him and looked at her lips. "That should be obvious. But you've just had a difficult day and you're vulnerable right now. I respect you too much to take advantage of the situation."

She fisted her knuckles in his hair. "What situation would

that be, Jake? Is it because we've spent practically every waking minute together for more than a week and I feel as if I've known you my whole life? Or because we're alone in a motel room and all you want to do is check the door locks? Or is it the fact that I'm falling in love with you?"

"You don't love me."

Becky sucked in her breath as she realized what she'd just said. She loved him? Of course, she loved him. The admission had slipped out so easily, she must have known it for days. Maybe weeks.

She loosened her grip on his hair so she could run her fingers through the unruly clumps. She loved his hair as much as his crooked smile and the laugh lines around his eyes. She loved his tenderness and his strength. She even loved the way he was determined to deny the possibility of love, because she knew why he was so cautious.

She slid one hand to his chest and put her palm over his heart. "I do love you, Jake. I love you enough to understand that most of your caution isn't for me, it's for you."

Beneath her palm, his heart was racing. Naked emotion sparked in his gaze. It wasn't only physical desire, it was a yearning for a connection that was more elemental than that.

Becky trembled from a shock wave of recognition. She knew that look. It was the same emotion she'd seen in the mirror. Jake longed for love as much as she did.

"Everyone left you, too," she said slowly. "It wasn't only Heather. Your brothers grew up and no longer needed you to take care of them. Your mother remarried and moved away. You loved all of them, but you ended up alone anyway. That's why you joined the army, wasn't it?"

"There were plenty of reasons I enlisted."

"Sure, but the main one was you were looking for a place to belong and for people who needed you. You loved your time in the army, didn't you?"

"I was good at what I did."

"Of course you would be. And you loved Heather, too. But then after your accident, you lost both. You were so hurt you gave up trying. That's why you don't let anyone get close to you. It's safer that way."

"It's not that simple."

"You're wrong. It *is* simple. You're the one who's making it complicated. You're a warm and caring person with a huge capacity to love, but you channel all your feelings into protectiveness because that's safe. That lets you keep your distance. It *makes* you keep your distance because it lets you ensure your relationships are temporary."

He pressed his lips together and eased her backward, breaking the contact of their bodies. "You're only focusing on me because your dream of being a Grosso didn't turn out the way you wanted."

She flung up her hands. "There you go again. You just proved my point. You're making excuses to protect yourself. First it was your age, then because we were working together, and now you're hiding behind this excuse of nobility."

"I should leave."

"And then what? I told you, I don't want to find my birth parents anymore. Your job is over. I don't need a detective or a bodyguard." She dropped her arms to her sides and stepped back. "I don't want you to be my protector. I want you to be my lover."

He regarded her in silence, his hands curling into fists. He clenched his jaw so hard, the tendons stood out on his neck. "There's nothing I'd like more, Becky," he said finally. His voice dropped to a low rasp. "I've tried, but I can't stop myself from touching you. I keep imagining how well we'd fit together. I fantasize about feeling the heat of your skin against mine, and I dream about you so vividly it surprises me when I wake up alone."

"Then why don't you stay with me?"

"Because you would want more than sex."

He was right. She wouldn't want just a night with him; she wanted a future, a lifetime, the very things that he'd claimed he didn't want.

But she hadn't believed him when he'd first told her that, and she still didn't. The yearning on his face spoke more powerfully than his words. "You want more, too, Jake. I can see it in your eyes. I feel it each time you kiss me. You might think we're different but deep inside we're the same." She swayed toward him. "You want to be loved as much as I do. That's why we recognized each other when we met. It's a bond we share that has nothing to do with our circumstances."

He closed his eyes and tipped back his head, his chest heaving.

"You can go on keeping your heart safe forever if you like," Becky whispered. "But why bother saving it if it never gets used?"

Jake turned to the door. Had she pushed him too hard? Becky pressed her knuckle to her mouth to keep from calling him back, but then she saw that he wasn't reaching for the knob.

Instead, he reached for the chain and slid it closed.

THE PETERS GIRL was as common as her mother, Cynthia thought, peering through the windshield. McMasters had stayed in her room all night. But then, many men had a weakness for tramps. Even Hank hadn't been immune.

She scowled at the gun on the seat beside her, clearly visible now that it was morning. It had been dark when she'd pulled into the parking lot. She hadn't anticipated needing to stay this long. Now that she was so close to finishing, the delay was frustrating.

It had taken hours to discover which motel they were registered at. She'd gone through the phone book until the desk clerk at this one had offered to connect her to McMasters's room. When Cynthia learned that Peters had her own room, she'd formed a foolproof plan. She would wait until the girl was alone before she approached her. Then she could take her someplace where no one would find the body and she could put this entire episode behind her.

That's what she should have done the last time, but she hadn't been thinking straight. She had been too eager to get back to Hank. But it had worked out anyway. No one had questioned her. No one had even suspected her role in the death. And this time the weapon she used would be far less clumsy.

Cynthia ran a fingertip along the barrel of the gun, then picked it up and slipped it into her handbag. She was getting tired of waiting. People were beginning to stir—she could see curtains pulled open at several of the windows and a few guests had already gotten in their cars and driven away. She couldn't remain parked here indefinitely. Perhaps she should simply break into the motel room and kill both McMasters and the girl…

Motion at the top of the staircase to the second story caught her eye. A tall, slim woman ran gracefully down the steps. She looked a mess. Baggy cargo pants flapped loosely against her long legs, a T-shirt with numbers on the front stretched over her chest and her streaked blond hair was a mass of tousled curls. In spite of the early hour, her face was radiant and a smile played around the corners of her mouth. She appeared as if she had just arisen from her lover's bed.

The Peters girl's resemblance to her mother was stronger than ever.

Cynthia was energized by a shaft of pure hatred. She clutched her handbag and got out of the car.

"I'D LIKE two honey-glazed and two chocolate-dipped, please." Becky did another scan of the shallow baskets that lined the wall behind the counter. "Oh, and two of the ones with the powdered sugar."

The teenage clerk yawned, displaying a mouthful of braces. "Raspberry or lemon?"

"What the heck, make it two of each."

He packed the doughnuts into a box and set it beside the cash register. "Anything else?"

"A bottle of orange juice and a large coffee."

"What kind of coffee?"

"Um, the eye-wobbler kind?"

He laughed and took one of the carafes from a hot plate. "Guess you have as much trouble waking up in the morning as I do."

Becky's cheeks burned as she thought of exactly how she'd woken up today. Daylight had barely begun to seep through the curtains when Jake had swept back her hair and kissed her neck. At the first touch of his lips she'd been wide awake, even though they couldn't have slept more than a few hours.

She had known Jake was in excellent physical shape, and he was mature enough to have the patience to take his time when he wanted something, but his skills as a lover surpassed anything she could have imagined. The night had flown past. She couldn't seem to stop smiling. Then again, she'd never been in love before.

Did Jake return her feelings? She suspected he did. The kind of passion he'd shown her had to spring from a source that was deeper than merely a physical attraction. She'd been right when she'd told him he had a great capacity to love. He might not have said the words, but he showed her how he felt in other, extremely delightful ways.

Now all she had to do was convince him it would last. Get him to drop the defensive caution of a lifetime. Show him his heart would be safe with her and she wouldn't change her feelings the way his fiancée had…

The euphoria she'd awoken with began to fade. As wonderful as the night had been, she and Jake still had a long way to go. He had trusted her enough to show her his scars, both the ones she could see and the ones she couldn't. She knew they weren't going to heal overnight.

"Ma'am?"

Becky started at the clerk's voice. A line had already formed behind her. She paid for the breakfast and left the coffee shop.

Her mind was on Jake as she walked back to the motel. He'd been in the shower when she'd left, and she was looking forward to surprising him with the doughnuts. She remembered how he'd brought breakfast the morning they'd met in Mrs. Krazowski's garage loft. Was that when she'd started to fall in love with him? Maybe. It was hard to choose one moment in particular since her feelings hadn't begun all at once. It had been more of a gradual accumulation.

She hoped it had been the same for Jake. The problems they'd already faced together added more layers to their relationship. They functioned well together, whatever they were doing. It was also a good sign that they could disagree without losing sight of the big picture.

Or was she only seeing what she wanted to see? What if Jake really didn't want her? What if he'd been feeling sorry for her, and had spent the night out of pity?

No. She couldn't let herself consider that. She knew what she'd felt when they'd made love. They'd made *love.*

"Miss Peters?"

Becky whipped her head around, shock leaving her momentarily speechless. She recognized the voice instantly, and it had the same effect on her this morning as it had yesterday afternoon. In spite of the warmth from the rising sun, she felt a chill across her shoulders.

Cynthia Shillington Brown was standing at the entrance

to the motel parking lot, looking much as she had the day before. As a matter of fact, she was still wearing her pearls and the same silk suit. But deep creases marred the front of her skirt and some of her hair had pulled loose from her French twist. As unlikely as it seemed, she appeared to have spent the night in her clothes.

Becky clutched the bag from the coffee shop against her chest as if it could offer her some protection, before she realized how silly it must look. She had no rational reason to dislike this woman, apart from connecting her to the loss of her dream of being Gina Grosso. "Mrs. Brown," she said. "What a surprise. I didn't expect to see you here."

"I was looking for you, Miss Peters." She looped the handles of a large handbag over her arm and gestured toward the parking lot. "Please, come with me."

"Why?"

"I told Daddy about your visit after you left. He does indeed remember your father and has agreed to see you."

Becky glanced around the parking lot. It was almost full. "Do you mean he's here?"

"No, Daddy's health wouldn't permit it. He's waiting for you at the house."

This didn't sound right. Would Gerald Shillington have sent out his daughter at dawn simply to convey a message? And why had she been waiting at the edge of the parking lot instead of contacting them by phone? Jake had left his card with her. His cell phone number was on it.

More than that, Cynthia's tone was flat, almost mechanical, but her eyes were too bright, as if she were running a fever. Becky's uneasiness grew. She started across the lot, heading for the staircase that led to her room. "That's great," she said. "I'll get Mr. McMasters."

Cynthia's heels clicked against the pavement as she kept pace beside her. "No, Daddy wants to see you alone, Miss

Peters. Just you. What he wants to tell you is confidential. It concerns your adoption."

Becky slowed her pace. So Jake and her father had been right. The Shillingtons did know about her adoption. What if Gerald really did want to see her? For all she knew, he might be eccentric enough to insist his daughter approach her this way. Another thought struck her. If Cynthia was actually her mother, as Jake had suggested, that might explain her demeanor. The prospect of exposure would be rattling her.

"He wants to tell you about your birth parents, Miss Peters."

She hesitated at the foot of the staircase. Why now, when she'd already decided to give up the search? She glanced at the bag in her hands, then looked up the stairs. She could see the window of her room from here. The urge to run to Jake was almost overwhelming.

Yet this could be her only chance to learn the truth of who she was. Where was the courage that Jake thought she had? So what if it did turn out that she was a Shillington? It would be better to know than to keep on wondering.

She looked at Cynthia. "All right. Please, tell your father I'll be there as soon as I can. I'm sure Mr. McMasters will be happy to drive me."

"You misunderstood. You must come with me now." She opened the clasp on her handbag, drew out a gun and pressed the muzzle to Becky's side beneath her ribs. "My car is the black sedan in the far corner beside the tree. I would like you to drive."

The bag from the doughnut shop dropped from Becky's fingers and split open on the bottom step, spraying coffee and powdered sugar on her pants. She barely noticed. She looked at the gun that was digging into her side. The fear she'd almost talked herself out of surged over her, freezing her in place.

This was crazy. It was broad daylight. The motel was booked to capacity because of today's race. There were dozens of potential witnesses. No sane person would think she was going to get away with this.

She looked once more at Cynthia's wrinkled clothes and her straggling hair, then focused on her face. The woman must be having a mental breakdown. There was no telling what she might do. "You're not well," Becky said. "Please, put the gun away."

"Don't be tiresome." Cynthia used the gun to nudge her backward. "I only want to talk to you. Come with me now and no one will need to get hurt."

"Mrs. Brown! This is a surprise."

At Jake's voice, Becky snapped up her head. He was standing at the top of the staircase, his feet bare beneath the hem of his jeans. His shirt hung open over his chest and his hair stuck out from his head in wet tufts. And he looked so good, so sane, in a world gone crazy that her knees buckled in relief.

But then she felt the sharp pain from the gun muzzle and her relief switched to fear. "No, Jake," she cried. "Go back. She's got a gun."

"Yes, I noticed that," he said evenly. His cane clunked on the staircase as he started down. "That's why I decided to join you. What's the problem, Mrs. Brown? You don't really want to hurt anyone, do you?"

Cynthia grasped Becky's arm and yanked her another few feet backward. "Stay where you are, Mr. McMasters."

"I'm sorry, Cynthia, but I can't do that," Jake said. He continued down the stairs, stepping past the splattered doughnuts. "Where Becky goes, I go. It's obvious you must have gone to a good deal of trouble to find us. What's on your mind?"

"It's the girl's fault. She's ruining everything. She's just like her mother."

Becky could see now that Jake was nowhere near as composed as he sounded. His knuckles were white where he gripped his cane. His entire body was so tense his movements were jerky. He kept his gaze steady on Cynthia with the concentration of someone approaching a rabid animal.

Was he trying to calm her? Stall her? Becky prayed he'd called the police before he'd come outside. "Her father wants to talk about my adoption," Becky said. "She wants me to go with her."

"Then we'll all go," Jake said. He followed, gradually closing the distance between them as Cynthia backed Becky across the lot toward a gleaming, black car. "I'd like to hear what Gerald has to say."

"This doesn't concern you, Mr. McMasters. This is between me and the girl."

"Well, no. Anything that happens to Becky does concern me, Cynthia. I happen to love her. Just as you love your husband."

What was Jake doing? Becky wondered. If this was an attempt to keep Cynthia calm, it wasn't working. At the mention of her husband, she'd jabbed the gun even tighter against Becky's side.

"You'll be well rid of her," Cynthia said. "You might have enjoyed yourself with her in bed but she's no good for you. She's like Amy. She'll ruin your life."

"I take it Amy is her mother's name?"

"Was. Amy Demille is dead. She can't hurt anyone now."

Pain knifed through Becky's chest. It wasn't from the gun. Her mother's name was Amy Demille? And she was dead? "What happened?" she asked. "Who was she?"

"She was nobody. Just a pretty face. She was always hanging around the tracks, fawning over Hank." Cynthia shook Becky's arm, her nails digging into her skin. "You're exactly like her. You came here only to torment me. It's your fault he left."

"Who left, Cynthia?" Jake asked, moving closer.

"Enough." Her voice was shrill. "Get in the car, Miss Peters."

Jake lunged forward to place himself between them and the car. "Not without me."

"Don't you understand?" Cynthia shouted. "It's all her fault. Once she's gone, everything will go back to the way it was. This will finally end."

"No, it won't end, Cynthia. I'll still be here. If you hurt Becky, I'll see you punished if it takes me the rest of my life." He leaned his cane against the car and held out his empty hands at his sides. His unbuttoned shirt flapped open in the breeze, exposing his bare chest as a target. "It looks as if you'll have to kill me, too."

Becky gasped. "Jake, no! Don't do this!"

For the first time since he'd appeared at the head of the stairs, he met her gaze. The facade of control he'd managed to maintain until now faltered and passion leaped to his eyes. He shifted, as if he were about to reach for her. Becky felt the pressure on her side ease as Cynthia swung the gun at Jake.

Before Becky could cry out a warning, he had pivoted on his good leg and used his stiffened forearm to deflect Cynthia's hand just as the gun went off. The back windshield of her car shattered in a starburst of tiny fragments. An instant later, Jake was gripping the gun and Cynthia was on her knees. He caught the back of her collar and twisted the fabric tight to hold her in place, then looked at Becky. "Are you all right?" he asked.

She passed her hand over her eyes, not surprised to see that her fingers were shaking. How many times had he asked her that question? How could she have been annoyed by it? And was it possible to love him more?

"Becky?"

"I'm fine." She blinked. She wasn't surprised to feel the heat of tears, either. Gradually, she became aware of sirens in the distance, drawing closer. And of voices all around them. She looked up. People were standing in the doorways along both floors. A crowd was gathering at the perimeter of the parking lot.

She returned her gaze to Jake. There were so many things she wanted to say, she didn't know where to start. She wanted to thank him for saving her life. And she wanted to yell at him for risking his. Most of all she wanted to plaster herself to the front of his body and feel the beat of his heart against hers and never let him go.

"I need to see Daddy."

At the muffled demand, both Jake and Becky returned their attention to Cynthia. She was sitting on her heels, her hands over her face. Only a few strands of hair remained in the twist at the back of her head. The rest straggled over her shoulders. "He'll help me. He always helps me."

Without loosening his grip on her collar, Jake thumbed the safety on the gun and tucked it into the back of his waistband. "It's over, Cynthia. The police are on their way."

"No, I have to go home. I have to be there when Hank comes back. He'll want to see me." Cynthia dropped her hands, revealing a face streaked with tears. She strained against Jake's grip, twisting to look up at him. "He has to come back. I did all of this for him. I love him so much. You must understand."

Becky looked from Cynthia to Jake. The things that had been said finally began to fall into place. The hate. The desperation. Even the madness made sense. She squatted in front of Cynthia to bring her face to her level. "Amy was my mother," Becky said. "And Hank Brown was my father, wasn't he?"

Cynthia's shoulders shook with the force of her sobs. "She was supposed to be gone. I convinced her to go. I told her Daddy wouldn't sponsor Hank if she was his girlfriend and she was standing in the way of his dream. She wanted him to be happy so she left. And he would have been happy. He turned to me. *Me.*" She slapped her chest. "I'm the one who really loved him. He saw that. He would have forgotten about Amy. But then she came back with *you* and would have ruined everything."

Only minutes ago this woman had meant to kill her, but Becky no longer felt fear when she looked at her. She felt sadness. Cynthia was falling apart before their eyes. "What did my mother do?" Becky asked.

"It was all her fault. She wanted to show him the baby. She said he deserved to know. She said he would marry her. She wouldn't go away. I picked up the lamp. I didn't mean to hit her that hard." She hugged her arms around herself and rocked from side to side. "Daddy helped me. It was raining so no one saw us put her back in her car. He gave the baby away. Hank never knew. Hank loved me. He loved *me.*"

A siren echoed from the street behind them. Tires screeched to a stop in the parking lot. Doors slammed, radios crackled and within seconds they were surrounded by police. Jake released his grip on Cynthia's jacket, reached into the pocket of his jeans and withdrew his cell phone. It was already on. Apparently it had been transmitting the entire time. "They're here," he said into it. "I'm hanging up now." He turned off the phone and put it away, then retrieved his cane and extended his free hand to Becky.

The danger was over, yet Becky still felt wobbly. There was too much to take in all at once. She'd come to Jake because she'd wanted to know who she was. Now she did. She wasn't Gina Grosso, yet racing *was* in her genes. She was the daughter of Hank Brown and his girlfriend, Amy

Demille. She hadn't been stolen or given away. Her father hadn't even known she existed.

Becky twined her fingers with Jake's and moved aside to make room for the police, but they hadn't taken more than a few steps away before Jake stopped between two parked cars and hauled her into his arms. "I'm sorry, Becky," he said, crushing her to his chest. "But I can't wait another second to do this. When I saw that gun—" His voice broke. He kissed her hard on the mouth until both of them were gasping for air. "I've never been that scared in my life."

"*You* were scared! What about me? How could you invite her to shoot you like that?"

"I meant what I said. I wouldn't have let her hurt you. I would have done anything. Love is worth any risk."

"Love?"

"Not the love Cynthia was talking about. That was sick. That was obsession." He drew her farther away from the crowd and kissed her again, then touched his forehead to hers and spoke against her lips. "I wouldn't have let you go. Even if you hadn't convinced me to stay, I wouldn't have been able to leave you."

"But I didn't—"

"I mean last night. You were right about everything. I was making excuses. I was afraid of opening my heart, but the thought of losing you…" He swallowed hard. "*That* scared the hell out of me."

Her mind reeled as she grasped what he was saying. "Jake?"

"I know this isn't the best time or place but I'm not taking any chances about this. I love you, Becky."

She didn't think her pulse could go any faster. It did. "Say it again."

He took her hand and placed it over his heart. "I love you. I never thought I'd find love again until you came along and showed me where to look." He smiled. "Some detective I am, huh?"

She'd almost been shot. So had he. Yet laughter was pushing past the sob that clogged her throat. Jake always knew just what to say.

And yes, it *was* possible to love him more.

EPILOGUE

THE INDIANAPOLIS TRACK thundered with the noise of cars racing full throttle. Less than five laps remained and anticipation shimmered in the air. The fans were on their feet. Those who hadn't yet shouted themselves hoarse added their voices to the din.

Becky stood on her toes to follow the action as Kent chased the pack around the bend. His last pit stop had cost him precious seconds and he needed to make up the time.

Jake moved to stand behind her and slipped his arms around her waist. "You're still cheering for Kent."

"Uh-huh. Even though I'm not a Grosso, I still want to see him win." She twisted her shoulders and smiled at Jake. "And considering the fact he got us these pit passes, it would seem ungrateful to cheer for the competition."

Jake's laugh rumbled through his chest to her back. "You're a true fan, Becky."

"I wouldn't have missed this for anything."

He arched one eyebrow. "Well, we did get here a little late."

She flushed and returned her gaze to the track. It was true, they had missed the start of the race. Thanks to Jake's quick thinking, most of this morning's confrontation with Cynthia had been recorded by the 911 operator, yet the police still had an endless list of questions. The reporters had been almost as persistent. Yet the reason Becky and Jake had arrived late was far more pleasant. Once they'd reached the privacy of their motel room, neither one had been in a hurry to leave.

Jake's scars *were* healing. He was talking freely about love and beginning to talk about a future with her. Yet it wouldn't matter to Becky if he never wanted marriage or children. The dream that she'd clung to was about love, and she loved Jake for what he was, not for what he could give her. From what she'd heard, Cynthia had made that mistake with Hank. In addition to beginning her marriage with an unthinkable deception, she'd tried to make her husband into something he wasn't. He'd already left her even before the truth had come out.

Cynthia was in custody for attempted kidnapping and it was only a matter of time before she would be charged in the kidnapping of baby Becky and the murder of Amy Demille. Once Gerald had heard his daughter had been arrested, he had made a confession of his own, revealing the rest of a thirty-one-year-old tragedy. Gerald maintained that Cynthia hadn't meant to kill Amy—she'd been waiting for Hank at his apartment when Amy had shown up with her baby. Nevertheless, Gerald had covered up his daughter's crime by cleaning up the apartment and helping her stage a car accident. It had been raining, so the police and everyone else had assumed Amy had died when her car had gone off the road. Gerald then had given the baby to Floyd Peters.

According to Gerald, the news of Amy's death had devastated Hank, who hadn't given up hope his girlfriend would come back to him. In his grief, he quit the Shillington team and didn't attend another race. Jake reasoned that Cynthia took full advantage of Hank's emotional vulnerability to move in on him, then counted on his gratitude to bind him to her for life.

Becky had new respect for Jake's determination not to take advantage of her emotional state, even though it had frustrated her at the time. At least he was no longer worried about her safety. Len had texted Jake that Ralph Bocci had been picked up by the border patrol only a few hours after Cynthia's arrest as he was trying to enter Mexico, and he was cooperating fully with the police. Jake had quickly realized there was no connection after all between his investigation of Becky's background and the murder of Alan Cargill, and he would call Lucas Haines tomorrow to let him know he'd been wrong.

One by one, the loose ends were getting tied up…except for Gina Grosso. If the real Gina was still out there somewhere, Becky was confident that Jake would eventually find her.

Movement near the corner of the pit box caught Becky's eye. She rolled her head against Jake's shoulder to see a tall, dark-haired man stride purposefully toward them.

Becky knew she hadn't met him before, yet she felt a jab of recognition. The way he moved was familiar somehow. So was the way he held his head and the shape of his blue eyes…

Her hopes soared. Was it possible? The police had told her they'd been trying to track him down to let him know what had happened, but she hadn't expected to see him so soon.

The man halted less than a yard away and stared at her with the shocked stillness of someone who was looking at a ghost.

Jake stiffened. He released her waist and was about to move in front of her when she stopped him with her hand on his arm. "It's okay, Jake," she said. "I think I know who this is."

"I asked around," the man said. "They told me you'd be with the Grossos, but I would have known you anywhere. My God!" He touched his fingertips to her cheek. His eyes filled with tears. "It's true. You look just like my Amy."

Becky's own vision blurred. All these years, people around NASCAR had said they recognized her. She'd thought it was because of her work, but the truth had been right in front of her all along. Amy Demille had been as much a racing fan as her daughter. She would have cheered for her boyfriend with the Shillington team. Her face would have been familiar to everyone who had worked on the circuit.

"I'm Hank Brown," the man said.

Becky smiled and stepped into an embrace that had been waiting for thirty-one years.

* * * * *

*For more thrill-a-minute romances
set against the exciting backdrop of the
NASCAR world, don't miss*

*RUNNING WIDE OPEN by Ken Casper
Available in October*

For a sneak peek, just turn the page!

HIS TAIL WAS SLIDING OUT from under him, the rear tires skidding to the right, up the steep bank of Turn Two. He'd told his crew chief he was running loose. Ethan assured him they'd fixed the problem. A wedge in the suspension during the last pit stop, his second, three pounds less air in the outside back tire, but it hadn't done the trick. If he could pull through this turn...

Bam!

Damn. Jem Nordstrom had just clipped his bumper. Intentionally? Probably, but it didn't make any difference. What was done was done. He was going into a full swerve now, veering up the side of the asphalt hill.

Two cars screamed past him on the inside, below him. The wall was behind him, above him, as he sailed into a counterclockwise rotation. Trey braced for the inevitable impact.

Bam!

Trey steered to the right in an attempt to regain traction. Not soon enough. Mitch Volmer smashed into him broadside. They plowed forward together down onto the straightaway, only the hood of Volmer's car separating the two drivers.

Another jolt. Volmer had been hit from behind. Like the last in a chain of marbles, Trey was set loose. Suddenly he was rolling sideways.

Over and over and over.

The tube-steel cage of Car No. 482, the snug fit of the

custom seat and the five-point harness kept him from being tossed around like the proverbial rag doll, but the bounces still weren't gentle.

Bang! Bang! Bang!

Then the direction changed and Trey felt himself flipping like a gymnast across an Olympic pad. One more rotation, this one in slow motion, then all movement ceased.

He was light-headed; no, he was upside down. Assess and act. He took a deep breath, started to release his harness and realized his left arm wasn't cooperating.

Broken? No pain. Not yet, at least.

He had to get out of the car. Hanging upside down wasn't good. Then there was the sudden panic of claustrophobia.

Fight the panic. Stay calm.

He struggled with his right hand to release the clasp. Click. He felt himself falling. On his head, but the helmet cushioned the impact. He writhed in the topsy-turvy world, aware of the overwhelming reek of raw fuel, of the heat encasing him. His left shoulder was beginning to hurt, to throb.

He tore away the net over the window, struggled to wiggle his way through the opening. His left arm, dangling, dragging, was producing serious pain now. On his back he squirmed, his right hand and arm pressed to the vertical side of the inverted car, to work his way out of the window opening. The pavement beneath him was hot and sticky, the acrid stench of asphalt and burned rubber scorched his nostrils.

He'd pulled his legs nearly free of the window frame when the first vehicle stopped close by. He rolled to his left to raise himself to his knees and nearly screamed as the pressure on his shoulder brought an explosion of pain.

Trey wasn't sure exactly when the stretcher materialized, but suddenly it was there. With excruciating slowness he was eased onto it and was bouncing across the rutted pavement.

He closed his eyes, feeling guilty about leaving other people in charge of what was happening to him.

"Is my arm broken?" he asked as the gurney was being pushed into the boxlike ambulance.

"We'll know in a minute. Try to relax."

A joker, obviously. Relax. If his arm was broken he'd be out for the rest of the season. There was too much at stake.

Trey's mental processes were beginning to clear. DNF. Did Not Finish. Damn. Not something he could afford with his point count already so low this far into the season.

The doors to the infield care center flew open and he was rolling inside.

"Curtain four," a female voice stated.

A very nice female voice. Confident and businesslike but not strident. Pleasant.

Trey rotated his head to the right. She was young, red-headed, wearing a white coat, a frown of concern on her pretty face. Blue eyes. Compassionate blue eyes. A man could—

She leaned over him. "I'm Dr. Foster. Tell me where you're hurting and what it feels like."

"Left shoulder," he said. They really were the most extraordinary blue eyes. "Dull ache now."

"Can you sit up for me?"

And beg? he nearly blurted out. "Sure."

The medic guided Trey's legs as he swung them over the side of the gurney and placed an arm across Trey's midback, carefully avoided applying pressure on his shoulder then helped lever him into a sitting position. For a second the room spun.

"Cut the shirt off," she directed the medic.

She took hold of his triceps and forearm above the wrist, folded the arm across his belly and studied his chest more closely. Her scrutiny shouldn't have surprised him, but the sensation of her perceptive eyes roaming over his bare skin suddenly felt intimate, making him uncomfortably aware of his rib cage expanding and contracting with each breath.

"That scar." She pointed to a nearly four-inch-long, pencil-thin line that ran vertically above his left pectoral muscle. "Do you have a pacemaker, Mr. Sanford?"

She raised her eyes and made contact with his. Oh, yes, he definitely liked looking into those cerulean-blue depths.

"There's nothing wrong with my heart, Doc," he murmured. "Trust me on that."

© 2009 Harlequin Books S.A.

HARLEQUIN®

||||| NASCAR®

Ken Casper
RUNNING WIDE OPEN

When an accident lands NASCAR driver Trey Sanford in the care of Dr. Nicole Foster, everything he's worked for is suddenly at risk. He will do whatever it takes to protect his family legacy…and his own carefully guarded secret. Nicole knows it would be tough for Trey to go public with his medical condition. He's already a hero to her kid brother. Maybe she can convince him that he is also a champion in her eyes.

Available October wherever books are sold.

www.GetYourHeartRacing.com

NASCAR18527

REQUEST YOUR
FREE BOOKS!

2 FREE NOVELS
FROM THE ROMANCE/SUSPENSE
COLLECTION PLUS 2 FREE GIFTS!

YES! Please send me 2 FREE novels from the Romance/Suspense Collection and my 2 FREE gifts (gifts are worth about $10). After receiving them, if I don't wish to receive any more books, I can return the shipping statement marked "cancel." If I don't cancel, I will receive 4 brand-new novels every month and be billed just $5.74 per book in the U.S. or $6.24 per book in Canada. That's a savings of at least 28% off the cover price. It's quite a bargain! Shipping and handling is just 50¢ per book.* I understand that accepting the 2 free books and gifts places me under no obligation to buy anything. I can always return a shipment and cancel at any time. Even if I never buy another book from the Reader Service, the two free books and gifts are mine to keep forever.

185 MDN EYNQ   385 MDN EYN2

Name	(PLEASE PRINT)

Address	Apt. #

City	State/Prov.	Zip/Postal Code

Signature (if under 18, a parent or guardian must sign)

Mail to **The Reader Service:**
IN U.S.A.: P.O. Box 1867, Buffalo, NY 14240-1867
IN CANADA: P.O. Box 609, Fort Erie, Ontario L2A 5X3

Not valid to current subscribers of the Romance Collection,
the Suspense Collection or the Romance/Suspense Collection.

Want to try two free books from another line?
Call 1-800-873-8635 or visit www.morefreebooks.com.

* Terms and prices subject to change without notice. Prices do not include applicable taxes. Sales tax applicable in N.Y. Canadian residents will be charged applicable provincial taxes and GST. Offer not valid in Quebec. This offer is limited to one order per household. All orders subject to approval. Credit or debit balances in a customer's account(s) may be offset by any other outstanding balance owed by or to the customer. Please allow 4 to 6 weeks for delivery. Offer available while quantities last.

Your Privacy: Harlequin is committed to protecting your privacy. Our Privacy Policy is available online at www.eHarlequin.com or upon request from the Reader Service. From time to time we make our lists of customers available to reputable third parties who may have a product or service of interest to you. If you would prefer we not share your name and address, please check here. ☐

BOB09